The Ice Cream Stand

and Other Stories & Poems
by 21 writers from The Place for Words & Workshops

Rhona Barlevy ◦ Marilou Barsam ◦ Bob Beckwith ◦ Karen Bella
Lisa R. Benson ◦ Charlotte Christen ◦ Linda Christen
Claudia A. Fox Tree ◦ George L. Hand ◦ Alma Hart ◦ E.M. Karrick
Jennifer Klein ◦ Lea Ann Knight ◦ Susan Miele ◦ Bruce Nickerson
Katherine Picard ◦ Mindy Pollack-Fusi ◦ Louise St. Germain
Kathleen Shure ◦ Dianalee Velie ◦ Judith Yarbrough

Edited by Mindy Pollack-Fusi

THE PLACE FOR WORDS PRESS
www.theplaceforwords.com

The Ice Cream Stand and Other Stories & Poems

The Place for Words Press

200 Great Road, Suite 254A, Bedford, MA 01730

Cover layout by Monderer Design www.monderer.com

ISBN: 978-0-9837397-0-8

DEDICATION

This book is dedicated to the memory and spirit of Jerry Christen, founder of Bedford Center for the Arts (BCA). Jerry's persistent vision of a community-wide arts identity for Bedford, Massachusetts was the force not only behind BCA but behind the emerging creativity of each of the authors in this book, whether they knew Jerry, or not. If it weren't for Jerry, The Place for Words & Workshops—an offshoot of BCA's "Write it Down" class—never would have become a reality. Thank you, Jerry; we miss you and are forever grateful for the many seeds you planted.

CONTENTS

ACKNOWLEDGMENTS

When the Bedford Cultural Council selected this book among its recipients of a Massachusetts Cultural Council grant, we were off and running to select the best works of 19 students and two teachers from The Place for Words & Workshops. Thank you to all involved.

Thanks also go to Bedford Center for the Arts for launching my class, "Write it Down," in 2007, and then supporting me as I moved it across town to my new writing center. I am grateful for our ongoing collaboration.

Thank you, too, to Dianalee Velie, who comes to The Place for Words & Workshops to teach poetry. The beautiful poems in this book were created with her guidance and prompts. We are honored that she submitted her poems, too.

Most important, I wish to thank my now-combined Tuesday and Thursday groups for trusting in me and in yourselves. And to our committee: Rhona Barlevy, Linda Christen, and Kitty Picard, for your hard work and support; Lea Ann Knight for guiding the publishing process; and Marilou Barsam for marketing advice. Also, my intern, Manya Wallace, for her help and ideas; Leslie Wittman for her web and proofreading skills; Pam Brown for legal counsel; and Monderer Design for our beautiful cover.

Finally, there would be no book if it weren't for my students taking a chance with me, a lifelong writer but new teacher who had a vision of one four-week class at BCA. That class has since evolved into a series of ongoing and new classes and groups, and more significantly, bonds forged among writers with deep souls, huge hearts and endless creativity.

--Mindy Pollack-Fusi

INTRODUCTION

The stories in this book stem from an introductory creative writing course. In each class, we build on key writing techniques, such as showing versus telling, using the five senses (see, hear, touch, taste, smell), voice, metaphor, building strong characters, addressing plot, pace, intrigue, dialogue, details and so on. We also do twenty-minute writing exercises in class to free the mind to create without judgment, calling on the subconscious to help us write from deep within. In an eerie way, if you're a believer, it might even be that we channel some muse from the great beyond…

To jumpstart my students' creativity, I provide writing "prompts." This book is organized, in the beginning, by common prompts assigned to my introductory classes. The most common prompts are writing about experiences: eating ice cream; in a car; finding a gray hair; the smell of Noxzema; thoughts of holidays. Sometimes prompts are miscellaneous words or images, or items in a secret bag. As this book progresses, you will notice that stories become longer; these are pieces by my long-term students whose work expands well beyond the basics of what can be produced in a twenty-minute writing exercise, or even in a homework assignment. Still, every story here began from a prompt—perhaps a photograph, a cluster of unrelated words, human characters created from animal calendar photos, or an assignment to write at a local coffee shop, observing those around you. (So far, no one has been arrested trying this last one!) We sometimes use nature as our prompt, creating nature metaphors to try to understand life's problems. I learned this technique at a wonderful annual workshop led by author Sheila Bender and her colleagues.

No matter the prompt, I know you will agree, the creativity that comes out of these classes is amazing. And if you follow the progression from short to longer stories, you will notice the writers' skill levels increase, too.

In the early sections of this book, we will mention the prompt via section headings. Later on, we focus only on subject matter. Just as an aside, you will not know, truly, whether a story is fiction or nonfiction. Also, occasionally, a poem mixes in with stories; these were poems written in prose classes, so we included them here. The section devoted to poems sometimes states the prompt, and sometimes does not, but all stemmed from prompts provided by the instructor, Dianalee Velie of www.dianaleevelie.com.

Now sit back, relax, and enjoy the stories and poems by these talented writers. You will laugh, you will cry, and you will be kept in suspense. Most of all, you will find this collection to be unforgettable, I promise!

--Mindy Pollack-Fusi

1

ICE CREAM

The Ice Cream Stand

By Bob Beckwith

How about some great midsummer entertainment for just $3.59? Come along with me as we go to the local ice cream stand on this warm, slightly humid Sunday evening. Drake's Farm is well known for its creamy smooth homemade ice cream. Ah—here we are now. Oh boy, lots of people here tonight enjoying their frozen treats and looking at all the farm animals.

I'll find a line that's moving right along, get my ice cream and then it's onto the show. Actually, the show begins the minute you drive in—it's called people watching. Ah, here we go, this line seems to be moving well—just three people in front of me. The first person is an older guy wearing glasses, dressed in a long-sleeved white shirt and dark brown slacks. He looks like he just came from taking the minutes at the Odd Fellows meeting. Let's call him Herbie. Certainly old Herb couldn't have too big an order—it doesn't look like he's the sociable type. Here comes the high school counter gal, Tootie Fruity, bouncing up to the service window with her blond pigtails and dressed in the company tee shirt that reads, "Drake's

Farm—Home of the Sweetest Cows." Between snaps on her gum, she asks Herbie if she can take his order. Herbie meekly says, "I'll have one chocolate, one vanilla and one strawberry. Tootie asks, 'Will that be cones or cups?" To which Herbie replies, "Three hand-packed half gallons." Oh man did I miscalculate this guy—he's *going* to the lodge meeting, not coming from it.

Ok, eight minutes later, Tootie is ready to help the couple just in front of me. All this time, while Herbie's order was being packed, this couple has either been reviewing the romantic moves they were using all weekend, or possibly practicing some new ones for the future. When Tootie asks for their order, they come up for air and reply, "Gosh we haven't had a chance to look at the menu." So now Tootie waits as they both read all the flavors—aloud. They finally settle on a banana split with vanilla, chocolate, and strawberry ice cream, all drenched in chocolate sauce and dabbed with whipped cream plus three red cherries on top. When Tootie delivers it, they ask for two spoons and a cup of water.

Finally it's my turn. I smile and tell Tootie, "I'll have a small cup of moose tracks." Tootie returns with a heaping cup. With bulging eyes I ask, "This is a small?" Tootie assures me it is. No wonder Americans are gaining so much weight! I pay my $3.59 and now I'm ready to check out the sights. I know what you're thinking—this over-the-hill guy is going to walk around and look at all the beautiful women in their short tank tops, shorter shorts and brightly colored thongs—on their feet of course. No, you're wrong—sometimes I look at other things too.

Let's go over here by the picnic tables and check out the action. Ah—here's a little old lady wearing a kerchief and flip-up sunglasses. She's dressed in a long-sleeved blouse—buttoned right up to her neck, and an ankle length skirt. She's sitting with her feet flat on the ground and her legs glued together. Wow I bet she's a live wire at a party. Let's call her Gertie. She's taking tiny, tiny bites from her cup of Black Raspberry. At the rate she's going, maybe I should offer her a soup spoon or a straw.

On my left is a guy who prefers talking with his hands—unfortunately he's using the hand with a double-scoop chocolate walnut fudge cone in it. He's got better action on that cone than a Salvation Army bell ringer. All his friends are running for cover while his melting ice cream is flying every which way as he punctuates yet another sentence.

Seated just in front of me is a four year old boy wearing a Red Sox hat and aviator sunglasses and trying to juggle a six-inch high chocolate/vanilla swirl cone. Obviously the summer heat is getting to it faster than he is. Right now his cone makes the Leaning Tower of Pisa look almost perpendicular. Oops—most of the swirl just landed in his lap. His comment? "Mommy, look what happened."

Well, finally, I have finished my "small" cup of moose tracks. Guess I'll mosey on over to the water bubbler for a drink before I head on home. My-my, I can't believe it—Herbie and Gertie are having a very animated conversation. I'll hang here a minute to see what this is all about. Let's listen. Herbie says, "How long has it been since we have seen each other?"

Gertie replies, "It was 1957, when you took me to the senior prom. I just moved back to this area last month from Chicago. What are you doing here?"

"I came out a little earlier to buy ice cream for our upcoming church social," Herbie replies. "After I delivered it to the church, I thought, gosh that looked so good I'll come back and have a cup." Then he asks, "Are you married?"

Gertie laughs. "No. I guess I never found anyone as sweet as you. And what about you?"

"My wife died about five years ago," Herbie replies.

Gertie removes her kerchief, fluffs up her hair. "How about if we get together sometime and catch up on old times?"

Herbie smiles wide. "That would just make my day—how about coming with me to the church social this Friday evening?"

"Oh that sounds like fun," Gertie says. They exchange phone numbers and Herbie agrees to call her soon—to just talk.

As they get ready to part company, Herbie smiles into Gertie's eyes, gives her a big hug and says, "I look forward to calling you."

Gertie flashes a sweet smile, and in a tender voice says, "I'll be waiting by my phone."

All this entertainment—plus some of the greatest homemade ice cream for just $3.59—what a bargain!

ꕤ

A Hot Fudge Sundae

By Judith Yarbrough

Call it strange, but I have never been a person that craved ice cream. However, on occasion, I have indulged myself in a hot fudge sundae. I prefer a tall, thin glass sundae holder, not a paper bowl, so that you can see what is going on as the sundae is made.

I am not a traditional hot fudge sundae eater, as I use strawberry ice cream instead of vanilla. I like being different and enjoy seeing the looks I receive when I ask for strawberry, such as those that imply the person is thinking, “Does this person really know how a hot fudge sundae should be made?” My reason for the strawberry really is that I find the sundae much more colorful with the hot fudge trickling down those strawberry mountains as it makes its way to the bottom of the glass sundae holder.

Next, I like a generous squirt of real whipped cream that makes it impossible to see the ice cream at the top. I almost have the urge at that point to start eating the whipped cream, but wait, it would not be complete without a few sprinkles of nuts and the perfect red cherry at the top.

I sit for a moment and look at this masterpiece before me. I pick up the long-stemmed sundae spoon, lightly touch the swirl of whipped cream, and smell the aroma of the hot fudge as it makes its way to my awaiting taste buds.

I feel at that moment like I am in heaven, but then that very last spoonful makes me feel so sad.

ꕥ

While We Ate Ice Cream

By Linda Christen

I scream you scream we all scream for ice cream! ~ Unknown

While we ate ice cream
Sitting with our love
Beneath the stars
On a clear summer evening

While we ate ice cream
Familiar rituals from youth
We loved we bonded
Our bubble was strengthened

While we ate ice cream
Laughing children climbed trees
Babies cried
Emissions mingled with bird song

While we ate ice cream
Grabbing extra napkins
Lick faster than the scoop can melt
Strong whimsical joy

While we ate ice cream
Filling our stomachs
Sweet smooth cream
Cools from within

While we ate ice cream
Others worked,
Some starved
And more people were murdered

While we ate ice cream
The world's pain was forgotten
We were refreshed
And life was beautiful

While we ate ice cream
We smiled

Eight Bowls

By Susan Miele

Rainbow sprinkles, fire engine red maraschino cherries, deep dark chocolate sauce dripping from the bottle, old fashion whipped cream, Brighams's ice cream, seven bowls, seven spoons and seven adorable faces waiting patiently to make their own ice cream sundaes at Grandpa's house. Well, eight bowls actually, as rarely did Grandpa skip an ice cream sundae himself. Crowded around the small table, their elbows touching and forearms itchy from the vinyl tablecloth—the patterns which changed each season—the kids could be heard from the dining room, sighing and exclaiming as they waited in anticipation for the first sweet, sugary cold bite of the sundae.

Ask any of his seven grandchildren to recall a fond memory of a time with their Grandpa, and most, if not all, will immediately say "ice cream sundaes at the kitchen table on Berkeley Street." The lingering smell of homemade tomato sauce hung in the air in the kitchen where the chatter was interrupted every so often by Grandpa's gentle teasing and admonishments, as little fingers grabbed for an extra cherry or maybe two.

Regardless of their current status—one in college, three in high school, one in middle school and two in grammar school—each one has a special place in their heart for the precious time they spent with each other and their Grandpa bonding over rather ordinary, yet extraordinary ice cream sundaes in the well-worn kitchen of my parent's well-worn home in their well-worn neighborhood in Somerville. The home they lived in for forty-eight years.

My dad is gone now, yet he's not; he lives on in the memories of rainbow sprinkles, fire-engine-red maraschino cherries and the hearts of each of his wonderful grandchildren who I doubt let a day pass without a happy thought of their much-loved Grandpa.

ꕥ

Ice Cream with Grandpa

By Marilou Barsam

The last time I had ice cream with my grandfather was on a hot summer day in August, one of those days where the humidity is so wet and the air so heavy your skin feels dirty and slimy even though you just showered ten minutes ago.

"Grandpa" was seventy-seven and I was twenty-three. He had been fighting off lymph node cancer and recovering from a pretty recent stroke—his illness interrupting the functioning of what had always been a very sharp mind—and quick wit, the extent to which I didn't realize in its entirety until that day…

As I typically would, I arrived at my grandparents' house mid-afternoon that Saturday—my car laden with dirty laundry which I preferred to take to the local Watertown Square Laundromat rather than the one close to my apartment in Chelsea, the latter never feeling quite as clean or inviting to me or my undergarments as the one in Watertown. In actuality, the real reason I chose the Watertown Laundromat probably had more to do with needing an excuse to visit my grandparents who I had emotionally hurt by leaving and venturing off to my first apartment. As they would often remind me, "You have almost no money and live with strange girl"—the latter being a co-worker that I had befriended at Jordan Marsh's advertising department where I had landed my first job in copywriting.

My grandparents—immigrants of Turkish/Armenia descent—had spent almost thirty years in this country, but never truly assimilated to certain cultural dispositions of America. One of these definitely was having raised me from age seven, only to see me so eagerly leave their safe and secure nest to fly off to a town which, as far as they were concerned, was at the opposite end of the country. And I was unmarried as well.

When I first arrived, I could see that my grandmother was not feeling well from the extreme heat, and she also seemed agitated with me. She half-smiled but still seemed sad when she said, "Suckus"—an endearing term in Armenian that means sweetheart—"almost two weeks we not see you. Are you all done with this house and us?"

I remember being so taken aback by her comment—not expecting it, although deep inside I knew that my departure had made this severe of an impact on her. I had always prayed that they could understand that I loved them both more than anything I could imagine. After all, they had saved me from living with "him," and from a life with my mother that was nothing less than turbulent and frightful for the three years I lived with them. In turn, my grandparents had given me every opportunity, including college, that they could barely afford with their meager income. With unconditional love, they had made up for all the neglect and abuse I had endured as a young child, yet I so needed to assert my independence and be sure I could make it without them. Could they understand this? Could they know that was the real reason I needed to go off on my own?

"Grandma, what a silly thing to say," I began. "I've just been so busy with work and getting the apartment ready—but now I'm here." We spent some time catching up, and then I remembered my laundry, so I asked them to come with me and suggested that we get ice cream while the clothes bounced around in the dryer.

My grandmother declined, saying it was too humid and she did not want to go far away from the house. But my grandfather said, "I come with you."

I didn't feel too badly leaving my grandmother, as I had planned to return and stay for dinner.

When we got to the Laundromat, my grandfather asked, "Why you not do laundry in our house?"

"Because, Grandpa, you don't have a dryer, and I don't like how stiff the fabrics feel when you hang them on the clothesline to dry." He smiled as if to say he knew, and then I said, "Wait here in the car, while I put my clothes in the machines, and then we can go to Friendly's."

Everyone else in Watertown was at Friendly's too, so much so that I could barely get a parking place. I rolled down all the windows, parked under a shady tree on a side street, and went to the takeout window to get our two cones—his, vanilla, and mine, chocolate with jimmies.

As we sat in the car, I watched as he slowly and purposely took each lick of ice cream, enjoying it tremendously but somehow looking too serious at the same time. Suddenly he stopped and did something I had only seen him do one other time in my life—the day we got the call that his sister, Rose, had died. He burst out crying, tears running down his kind and stroke-sagging cheeks, struggling to hold back the soft sobs as he swallowed his last licks of ice cream.

"Grandpa, what's the matter, why are you crying?" I blurted out.

"Because, Yavroom"—another Armenia term of affection for me—"I come to tell you I die soon and you need to be ready. This is why Grandma and I so sad you not live with us. This is why we miss you so much."

"Grandpa, no one knows exactly when they will die. Why are you saying this?" And now I, too, joined him in crying—big wet tears falling fast and furious down my cheeks, their salty wetness co-mingling with the melting chocolate streams slowly dripping down my sugar cone onto my fingers. All five fingers clenched desperately around the frail wafer of a cone, as if holding on tightly would somehow ensure that he would not ever die and leave me.

"It's alright, Yavroom, I have some time left, but not much. It's alright darling, don't be too sad. I understand someday everyone has to die and I understand that I am finished."

He handed me his cone and I threw both cones outside into a barrel next to my car window. I wiped some remaining chocolate off my right cheek and he smiled at me with that sweet stubbly hair-covered face of his. As I pressed my face against his and hugged him ever so tightly, all I could think of was how many more ice creams I might be able to have with him before his end really came, and wondering if that was a stupid thought to have at a time like this…

ഇരു

2

CARS

Red Ones Go Faster

By Katherine Picard

Red ones go faster! Or so all of us who owned sports cars in the late '60s/early '70s have been known to say. If you had a red car, the color was often referred to as "ticket-me-first" red! Surveys even revealed that red cars are perceived to be going faster. As a result, those of us who had red cars watched the speedometers and the rear-view mirrors more closely.

Even car design influences our perception of speed. Take tail fins—the exaggerated tail fins, bullet-shaped tail lights, Cadillac fins—the term FINS itself. Even fish. The shark—known for its speed—is readily identified by its fin!

But I digress. My first "red" car was a brand new 1967 red MGB! It replaced my used, but loved, white 1960 MGA. Shortly after I bought this car, I started dating my to-be husband. He had a white Chevy II (his first car). The joke was that I married him for his car. My MGB was my fourth car, following my basic beige Renault

Dauphne, a jazzy green Studebaker Silver Hawk (which had great fins), my used white MGA, and then my shiny, new Red MGB. Love at first sight!

We got married, eventually sold the Chevy II and kept the MGB. Our son, Steve, arrived on the scene and was able to sit in the boot for a while, sharing space with the bags of groceries. However, when our daughter, Nicole, arrived, space became a premium with her on my lap, Steve in the boot, and four bags of groceries. We had outgrown the car. We bought a VW square back (translate to station wagon; I can still recall the mental adjustment I had to make to go from jazzy cars to— heaven forbid—a station wagon. At least it had a sun roof!).

I put an ad in the paper and some young guy came to look at the MGB and could hardly contain his excitement. I practically had to sign an affidavit stating that I would not sell it out from under him. I couldn't do that—I recognized the signs of love at first sight, and you can't deny anyone the rush that comes with that.

After many years of being a one-car family, and the shuffling around of people and locations that involves, we bought a used Renault from one of my students. Eventually, I got another car to call my own. Again, it was used, a 1984 Toyota Celica. But if you ask me the color I'd have to say, "Red, of course."

Now I drive a gray 2004 Saab four-door sedan! Nice car! Used, but it has leather interior, and all the extras. I console myself with the belief that car makers don't make a nice "red" anymore. Not like the old red!

ꕥ

The Rambler

By Bruce Nickerson

Only New England fall Saturdays could be this beautiful, with leaves turning all sorts of harlequin colors, the air crisp but not cold, and smoke in the air as neighbors burned piles of leaves. It was a day meant for a high school senior to take his girlfriend for a ride in the family car with its top down.

It was a four-year-old Nash Rambler, not a "cool" car. To offset the Rambler's dorkiness, I perfected the art of making tires squeal when starting: rev the engine, then pop the clutch. It was hard on tires and drive train, and on my father's nerves. But it got attention in a real cool way.

I could borrow the car as long as no one else needed it. It had to be returned with a full tank of gas, at twenty-six cents a gallon.

"But what if it's almost empty when I get it?" I asked.

"That's the rule." My father's rule of course. He made all the family rules.

"Can I borrow the car?" I asked my mother since my father was out for the day.

"What for?" Mom asked.

"I want to go for a ride."

"With who?" Another rule: Who, where, when, and so on.

"Peg."

"Where you going?"

"Arnold Arboretum." The Harvard facility would be beautiful on such a fall day. Then maybe an ice cream at Howard Johnson's if I had enough change left over from filling the tank.

"Ok, be home for supper." Mom smiled. Memories of a long past courtship?

"Ok."

"Remember, don't put the top down. It has to be fixed. When it's down we can't put it back up." Mom was the peacemaker between Dad and me, and she wanted to make sure there would be no fuss about the car.

"I'll remember," I tossed back at her as I ran out the door.

I drove the few blocks to Peg's house. We met at a joint Boy Scout/Girl Scout (our "Ladies Auxiliary") social. She was a year or so older than I, a senior at Somerville High School. I went to a religiously conservative Protestant school. She lived with two older people, whom she called Dad and Mum. They were her adopted parents, and I never got more from Peg than that she was the child of "the town drunk" as she put it. She never mentioned her mother. We were both bright and near the tops of our classes academically. We dated for almost six months before I got up enough courage to kiss her. But never with my tongue in her mouth.

I parked the car in front of the house, and turned off the key. I got out of the car. I walked to the door. I rang the bell. Another rule: "If I ever catch you sitting in the car outside a girl's house and honking the horn rather than going to the door and ringing the door bell, you won't drive again for at least a month." And I was to walk her to her door when bringing her home. "AND don't let me catch you giving her your class ring," he'd say, referencing a practice back then amongst teenagers when going steady.

I really did obey the rules, or most of them.

Peg came down the flight of stairs from the second floor where the family lived, opened the door, and smiled at me with her dark eyes. "Hi."

"Hi. Want to drive to the Arnold Arboretum?"

"That would be really nice. Just let me tell Dad and Mum where we're going and when we'll be home, right?"

"Ok."

She went up the stairs, and I heard a few voices. She came down the stairs again and I escorted her politely to the car, started the car, and off we went. No tire squealing. Be a nice boy.

It was a glorious afternoon indeed, exactly as I had hoped: Bright sunshine, colorful leaves, a walk through the Arboretum hand-in-hand, kicking rustling leaves, a kiss or two through our mutual shyness, then a stop at Howard Johnson's for two ice cream cones. The outing was made even more wonderful with the convertible top down, the wind in our faces and Peg's curly, short dark hair blowing in the car's slipstream.

We were back by the required four p.m., and I stopped the car in front of Peg's house, opened the car door, and walked her to her front door where she—hallelujah—gave me a hurried, furtive kiss: "Don't want Mum and Dad to see." She opened the door and disappeared inside, and I heard her footsteps climbing the stairs, imagining myself behind her, watching the movement of her legs beneath her slacks and the sway of her hips.

I drove the few blocks home, parked the car, and tried to put the top up. I tried again. I opened the trunk to fiddle with the top mechanism and got my hand rusty and greasy on the recalcitrant mechanism. "Ah well, get some tools from the cellar, fiddle some more, and it will be fixed before Dad gets home," I thought.

I looked up and saw him walking toward me down the cinder paved driveway between the houses, each step like an angry march, and his face couldn't hide his annoyance. He had gotten home early and had seen the car parked out front with its top down.

I sensed him follow me into the house. My mother stood in the narrow darkening hallway at the base of the stairs going up to the bedrooms on the second and third floors, right next to the dark walnut newel post, the stained glass window above at the turn of the stairs, her hand resting anxiously on top of the post, a worried look on her face. The aroma of that night's pork and beans wafted from the kitchen behind her.

"Well," he exploded loudly. My mother cringed and shrank back against the wall. "So you had to show off for your girlfriend!"

"It's a nice day for a convertible ride with the top down. That's what it's made for."

"I told you not to put the top down," he raged.

I pushed past him to start up the stairs. He stepped towards me. My mother put a hand on his arm. "Bernard, he's just a boy."

"But old enough to drive a car and disobey his father," he continued, storming. His voice increased a number of decibels; his face grew redder as his annoyance turned to anger.

"Well, if we had a car that worked like it should…." I started.

Mom said, placatingly, "Well it's what we could afford…"

I glared into Dad's angry eyes: "If you had a decent job we could afford a real car instead of that shitbox…"

He stepped back, moved his right leg behind him slightly for leverage, and started to swing a kick. I turned, grabbed his ankle, twisted, almost toppled him. My mother stepped between us and pushed us apart. I turned my back on him, started up the stairs, stopped halfway near the stained glass window, its colored light on my face. I turned, looked him in the face, and with a voice dripping sarcasm said, "So you're not man enough to use your hands?"

I turned and walked slowly to my room.

ഇഗ

Stop Sign Stop Sign Stop Sign

By Rhona Barlevy

Sharon could feel the pulsing idle of the car's engine as she and David sat in the endless bumper-to-bumper traffic. It was hot out, and the searing sun was causing heat waves to ripple off the tops of the glaring car hoods. Sharon closed her eyes in hopes that by avoiding the glare she could avert the already piercing headache she felt coming on. It was the kind she always got when she felt panicked, a piercing pain that started over her left eye and radiated down her face, like the sharp sizzling white hot patterns lightening makes across the sky.

Ucch! Sharon thought, just what I need, a migraine, endless traffic and a visit with my mother, all in the same evening. She glanced over at David who, as usual, seemed oblivious to the misery of the whole situation. He just sat humming to some melancholy Frank Sinatra song on the radio while beating out a rhythm with his thumbs on the steering wheel. David's face was relaxed and his springy black curls lay damp around his face from his recent shower. The cars ahead of them started to move up and David shifted the car into gear and rolled a few feet ahead. Sharon could now see farther up the street and there appeared to be no relief.

"What are we going to do?" Sharon whined. "We'll never make it to dinner on time!" David turned slowly, his face with the vague bleary expression of someone who had just suddenly been woken up. After a few seconds, he focused on her and, with that edgy condescending voice he sometimes used, said, "Well you could actually take your cell phone out of your bag, turn it on and call your mother and tell her we'll be late. I know that's a novel idea but it just might work."

"Ha ha," Sharon said as her face flushed with growing anxiety and irritation. "You know what she's like, she'll think I did this on purpose. She'll find some way to blame me for being late."

"Look, Sharon, what would you like me to do?" David said, his voice rising with his own irritation. "It's rush-hour traffic and there is probably some accident up ahead and we are stuck here! I don't know which is worse, your Mom's bitchiness or your hysteria. JUST CALL!" Sharon did not answer him, but David could see tears watering the edges of her eyes as she slowly bent down to retrieve the cell phone from her bag on the car floor. Feeling like a shit, he reached over and gently squeezed the hand she held tightly fisted in her lap. "I'm sorry," he said. "I know how difficult and unreasonable she can be. I have an idea. Let's do what Dr. Greenblatt suggested and role-play it before you call."

"Oh David." Sharon's voice came out almost as a wail. "I don't really find that it helps, it just makes me feel stupid."

"Well let's just try," David said. "I'll be your Mom. Brinnng! Brinnng!" David said imitating the phone, and then in a high falsetto voice said, "Hello." Sharon sat, not responding. "Oh come on, Shar, just try it, David pleaded.

"Okay," Sharon mumbled, as a faint tear wandered down her cheek and she sniffled. "Hello, Mom, it's me. I'm afraid we're stuck in really bad traffic and we are going to be late. Some sort of accident I think. We are at Grant and Westminster Streets right now. I think we may be another half-hour."

"Well, Sharon," said David, continuing in his exaggerated voice, "Don't you think you could have planned this a little better? You should have gone the way I told you. Now if you want to get here on time, I suggest you and David get out of the car, lift it up and carry it three blocks beyond Grant Street to Dover, then drive for four blocks, make a left on Hemlock, a right on Selden, a left on Grey, a right on Evans to Lowell Road. Go to the end of the road, it's a dead end, then lift the car up again and go through Mrs. Gallardo's backyard and you'll be here. I don't see what the big deal is!"

By now Sharon had dissolved into giggles, her whole body shaking with them. David loved her giggles, they sounded like tinkling glass and jingle bells. "Oh, David," Sharon said between giggles, "I'm not sure that's the kind of role playing we're supposed to do, but it's working."

Suddenly, from behind, a car honked and David looked up to see that the traffic had moved a few car lengths. The mood broken, David turned to Sharon and quietly said, "You really need to call."

"I know," she sighed and started dialing the number. "Hello, it's me. We're going to be late. There appears to be some sort of accident and the traffic is really backed up. What, oh, maybe a half-hour...Okay I'll call when we get closer. Bye." Sharon returned her cell to her bag and sat back smiling. David turned and looked at her with wide-eyed surprise. "Wow, that role-playing really works better than I thought.

"Don't be an idiot," Sharon giggled. "I just got lucky and my Dad answered the phone. I'm sure we'll get an earful from Marion-the-Martyr when we get there." David gave a knowing nod as he once again shifted the car and rolled a few feet ahead. "I wonder how many times she will tell us that the wonderful dinner she made is ruined because she had to reheat it?" Sharon said a little more seriously.

As the car inched forward, Sharon could more clearly see the larger intersection of Grant and Westminster Streets. Right now there was a policeman controlling the traffic, but usually that fell to the four stop signs that guarded each corner. Sharon had never really paid much attention to them, but now their intense, luscious red color held her eyes. Perched as they were on long bright green poles, they looked like surrealistic lollipops. The white, almost neon luminescent word "stop," written in the middle, seemed to flash on and off. Dr Greenblatt had suggested to her, in a recent session, that she try visualizing this word when her anxious thoughts began taunting her like nasty little children. She had tried it, but had not found it useful, because her mind just bounced around. But maybe visualizing these stop signs would work. So as she sat in the bumper-to-bumper traffic, Sharon closed her eyes and began to practice calling forth the vivid image of the stop signs.

Thirty minutes later, David and Sharon were pulling up in front of her parent's house. David leaned over and kissed Sharon's cheek, "I have your back you know."

"I know," she responded and kissed him back. They got out of the car and started to walk up the red brick path, but before they had even taken more then a few steps, the door sprung wide open. There framed in the door way was Marion-the-Martyr. She had that pinched bitter look on her face, and she was already yelling about how her wonderful dinner was ruined. Sharon started to feel her migraine start up again, and in a panic began screaming in her head STOP SIGN STOP SIGN STOP SIGN! Then all of a sudden laughter erupted from deep inside of her, and she turned to look up at David to see if he thought this was funny too. But he was not laughing; instead, there was a look of serious concern on his face. Sharon was puzzled until she realized she was sobbing, not laughing, and streams of tears were running down her face. Well, so much for stop signs she thought.

ꕥ

The Universe Remembers

By Claudia A. Fox Tree

The steel-blue Suburban, with rust along the outside and open holes in the inside corners, quietly whistles down Route 128. Five little voices… no, five *screaming* voices… no, some quiet, some screaming, all break the monotonous silence.

"What is going on in the back seat, don't you know I'm trying to concentrate on the road and not get into an accident?" I ask.

The Pow Wow was fun, but my weary legs and sore back remind me of the packing, unpacking, and repacking I had to do to so we could spend the three days in Topsfield. Setting up the booth to sell the hand-crafted clay jewelry took most of the first morning. Then dressing us all in our regalia to dance took up most of the afternoon. The drum kept the Earth's heartbeat steady as its singers honored the plants and the animals.

In the evening, as mosquitoes sang their bothersome tune and stung in sensitive spots, there was camp to set up. Unraveling the tent and sleeping bags is a parent's comeuppance for when they were children and loved to camp. (Meanwhile, *their* parents were doing the heavy lifting, cooking, cleaning, and "kitchen is now outdoors" stuff.) Thirty-six hours later, the process reversed itself. The oldest child is indentured to help, complaining that they must stuff sleeping bags in hell. The reservation-ready vehicle is more packed than when we left, because nothing ever fits quite the same or as comfortably on the way home.

Now, traveling home, everyone wants to play the flute we had just traded for green frog skins, but only one youngster is holding it. "You're no good," says one to the other, who replies, "You're a jerk, too."

Through the din of children, a tired-yet-strong, quiet-yet-forceful, calm-but-certainly-commanding voice comes out of me. "You know that everything mean you do to another person comes back to you. The universe remembers. How do you think that living flute in your hands feels? That tree gave its arm so that another arm attached to a crafter's hand could carve it into an instrument. Now it absorbs the emotion you are sharing with it."

"You're making that up," say two of five back to their mother.

"Just play it," say I, with wisdom to know what would happen and fear that it might not.

So the one takes the cedar stick that is longer than her arm and places the shiny, smooth end to her lips. Quiet surrounds us, except for the noise of the road as we ride along slowly, almost in silence. Finally... whoooooooo, thwooooooooo emanates from the seat with the one who was breathing air and life into that limb of the tree, carved for this very moment—a lesson in the making. I say, "What do you think of that sound coming from that flute now?"

A sob. "It's very sad. We shouldn't have fought."

ꕥ

A Few Groceries

By Bob Beckwith

My wife called me at my office on a hot, muggy summer afternoon and asked if I would pick up a few groceries on the way home. I was up to my ears in work, but being the good husband I said, "Sure, what do you need?" Besides, I found our marriage works far better when I compromise and do what she asks.

One item she requested was boneless chicken breasts. After purchasing all the groceries, I put them in the trunk of my car and promptly drove home. I guess I had remembered all the items on her list, since no mention was made of anything missing.

The following afternoon I got back into my car and noticed a rather odd smell. I opened the windows and promptly put the smell out of my mind. The next day when I got into my car, the odor was ten times worse. All I could think was, *"Who died in here?"* Being in a hurry for a meeting, I again put the windows down and drove off.

Later, when I returned to my car, the smell was downright raunchy. At that, I opened the trunk and discovered a package containing chicken bones, which I had not requested from the butcher. After that, I nicely informed my wife that perhaps it would be best if she did the shopping.

ꕥ

The Ride Age 8

By Marilou Barsam

His oily, black, slicked-down hair was all I could see of my stepfather's head from the back seat.

Next to him sat my mother, giggling as usual at what seemed inappropriate then; although I was too young to even know the word "inappropriate," my little girl sense and my quivering stomach were telling me that something was not right.

With each lurching movement of the car, my mother would laugh, and the mass of her curly long brown hair would bounce up and down, as if mimicking the bouncing of the car as it too bounced over bumpy gravel and rocks in the road.

Only my grandmother, sitting next to me in the back seat, seemed as afraid of what he was about to do—her body slowly sinking, as mine was, as we realized we had no control over him and hoped silently that he would not hurt us.

Suddenly I heard him say, "You wanted a good view—well here—how's this one?"

And as he said that, grinning through his words, he began to poke his foot at the accelerator, teasing it and me, back and forth, poke-poke, each time bringing us further and closer to the very edge of the mountain's outlook point; each time reminding me that I could not stop him and that soon we may all be tumbling down past the big rocky slopes into the wide mouth of the green canyon below.

And then without a moment's notice, the car seemed to be tipping on its head, peering with its big black headlight eyes into the hole below.

My grandmother yelled, "Henry, please stop," and she prayed to God in Armenian. My mother giggled. I started to cry and scream, "Stop, stop I don't like this!" My mother then said a bad word in French.

All he did in return was laugh at us as he turned his black shiny head sideways with a devil grin on it, to make sure he had scared us all, and then a big whooshing scratchy noise and we were going backwards at 100-miles-an-hour with dust flying all around us, through the opened windows, into our eyes and up our nostrils. I began coughing in an attempt to resist the dust sweeping down into my already dry and parched throat.

This enraged him, and as he screamed at me for being such a baby, he spun the car into what I would come to learn was a "wheely," and at that point I vomited all over the seat in front of me and all over his big black head. I don't remember the sequence of events except for a lot of yelling, his grabbing my arm and yanking me out of the back seat, a lot of commotion over the mess I had made, and my grandmother crying.

And then, I do remember, my stomach relieved of its contents, closing up tight into a small ball, my eight-year-old mind registering for the first time that my stepfather was bad.

As we drove home, there was dead silence in the car. And with that silence something in me died too, as all hopes that I would be happy settling in California with my mother and stepfather, far away from my grandmother and grandfather, slowly wilted away.

ꙮ

3

THROUGH THE AGES

My First Gray Hair

By Lea Ann Knight

I carefully peer into the full-length mirror in my dressing room, a sanctuary away from the noise and chaos that reigns in the other rooms of my house. Despite being bleary-eyed from lack of sleep, I can still see the toll this ongoing stock market meltdown has started to take on my reflection. Or perhaps the mirror is starting to warp?

Stepping closer in the dim light (after all, who wants a bright light and a mirror at age forty-seven?), I catch a flash of something on my head. Was that a piece of down from the pillow that had cradled my tossing and turning head all last night? Was I about to go to work with pillow fluff in my hair? I quickly begin combing through the individual strands in search of the elusive object that reflected off the light moments earlier. Frantic, I realize that I am now going to be late to work, where there will inevitably be more concerned and anxious voice mail messages awaiting my arrival today. And yet, I am reluctant to leave the mirror until my hair, at least, is under control.

And there it is again—that flash in the amber light of the overhead lamp. I stop combing and gently part the strands of hair where the flashing culprit is hiding. Could it be? "No, no," I moan, crumpling to the carpeted floor in defeat. It has finally happened; my first gray hair. One single strand, waving proudly in the middle of my forehead, declaring that stress has finally manifested itself in the color of my coiffure.

A badge of wisdom, some would say. To them I reply, NEVER! I will not let the stock market take the color from around my face. As I rise from my oasis floor, I am not yet defeated. I brush my hair one last time, straighten my suit and march proudly to the telephone. I take a deep breath and smile, knowing that my colorist and my broker are both on speed-dial.

ꙮ

I Found a Gray Hair Today

By Bruce Nickerson

I found a gray hair today. But the wrinkles are not there yet. Skin still taut and firm. And in spite of the gray hair, the rest of the hair still has its youthful fullness and sheen. The exercise helps—riding the bike to and from work twelve miles each way keeps the legs in shape. And the abs.

One gray hair? Not what one usually thinks—probably just a normal variation in the coloring, not a harbinger of approaching senility.

Will anyone else notice? Should I pull it out? I think not. It hurts too much. Reminds me of Hawthorne's "Birthmark" and the little pygmy hand.

Best leave it alone. After all, as Herrick said "A slight disorder in the dress kindles in me a wantonness." And that one gray hair could well be an intriguing beauty mark. After all, one has to be quite close to see it, and when that close the beauty of the whole overwhelms such a slight imperfection. How philosophical! The fault can reveal the perfection!

But I still will not tell my wife she has a gray hair.

ꙮ

Graying Eyebrows

By Mindy Pollack-Fusi

I found a gray hair today. I can't believe it. A friend in her sixties once said that her eyebrows were still brown even though her hair was half gray. But what's this? I look in the magnifying mirror today to pluck my eyebrows, and there's a gray eyebrow hair! The hair on my head is probably only twenty-five percent gray—not that I'd know anymore. I've been coloring it for nearly ten years, most of that time doing it myself, the low-cost way, with eight-dollar Lady Clairol, the kind that washes out eventually. Last month, following a friend's advice, I splurged and spent sixteen dollars to buy two colors that I mixed together. That way, as my friend advised, you don't find yourself at a dinner party looking at your neighbor and thinking, "Damn, she's wearing Midnight Brunette too," or, "Wow, I like the way Maroon Mama looks on her better than on me."

But back to my white eyebrow hair. It's like a black dog with one white spot on him but, in dogs, that's endearing! For me, it's just a sign that deterioration is on its way. No doubt, one white hair will turn into two, two into three, and so forth. So I took control. I plucked this one out! But if I keep plucking when more appear, will I have any eyebrows left when I'm done? Will I need to be like those old ladies in the senior center, or maybe more like those has-been, aging movie stars like Zsa Zsa Gabor, who draw a heavy line with eyebrow pencil and think it's fashionable, when it's really just foolish?

I guess at some point I will have to come to grips with white eyebrows, just as I will have to cope with those lines surfacing around my eyes that no longer hide behind what the cosmetic companies call "concealer." Really, what do they conceal—
that I don't have my youth anymore?

ꕥ

Who is that Woman?

By Rhona Barlevy

I found a gray hair today, and yesterday and the day before that. Who is this jowly-faced gray-haired woman staring at me from the mirror? She's making all kinds of faces I don't recognize. I wish she would stop and go away! It's easier if I don't wear my glasses. Then she looks younger, with fewer lines, and the gray blurs to brown. Sometimes I think it's my mom looking back, or my dad, and even my grandmother, but it certainly isn't me.

Years ago when I worked in a hospital, I encountered a perceptual disorder caused by strokes and other neurological conditions. Agnosia it was called; the inability to recognize people's faces, objects and so on. The noted neurologist Oliver Sacks wrote a book about such things called *The Man Who Mistook His Wife for a Hat.* I believe there is a chapter about me in that book called, *The Woman Who Could Not Recognize Herself in the Mirror.*

Sometimes I like to sneak up on the mirror, then turn quickly to surprise myself and see if I know the woman who is looking back. It never works; I still can't tell. Other people look like themselves to me, mirror or not. Why am I not getting this? Will I die not recognizing myself? When looking back at old childhood pictures, I can still recognize that little person and feel her inside. On occasion, she even peeks out from the mirror. Which is all very sweet, but it still leaves me with one big question: Who the Hell is that Woman in the Mirror?!

༄༅

A Gray Hair

By Judith Yarbrough

I found a gray hair and I thought these were supposed to be a long way off. My mom had started to gray early, but in as much as I had my father's looks and a good head of dark hair, how dare they start now? I was just getting out of college; how could I possibly deal with this tragedy?

I immediately went to my hairdresser the next day—fortunately a family friend, so no appointment necessary—and spoke with him. I only went for a haircut on occasion, but, gosh, was I going to have to add coloring now to these visits?

Sitting nervously in his chair, I put my finger on the gray hair on the top of my head and said, "Enzo, what do you think?"

He looked and looked and finally said to me, quite emphatically, "What am I looking for?"

"Can't you see it," I said. "This gray hair is sticking right out."

He looked at where my finger was pointing. "Well, I don't think it is cause for alarm."

"But my hair is so dark, you can't miss it," I said.

Enzo replied, in his wonderful Italian voice, "Bella, your face is so lovely, no one will ever notice that gray hair."

I was so glad I had gone to see him; Enzo always knew what to say. As I left the shop, I said to myself, "Who cares, I will pull it out when I get home."

ജ്ഞ

Beach Day!

By Linda Christen

Late May and the sun is crisp, shining bright
Clear dry air, perfect day for going to the beach.
Quick morning phone calls
Excuse notes scribbled and we're flying in the beige bomb
Headed up Route 128 to the sugar sands of Good Harbor.

Once there we begin the sacred tanning ritual.
First baby oil, Johnson's baby pink smell reminiscent of gentle moments.
Douse it thickly over legs, arms, neck and chest, glisten.
Lie back, close your eyes, tune in to the dusty hot sand
Squawking of sea gulls, repetitive rushing of surf heading out to sea

Rays soaking skin, eyelids filtering a spotty color show
The heat makes me lightheaded, groggy
Thick consciousness, rollover
Sleep lightly as the sun fills you on this long carefree baby oil day
Sedate ride home, energy evaporated by the baby oil bake.

Later that night, prickly skin
Eucalyptus salve melts into my Solarcane epidermis.
Plum colored; cotton top a grade two sand paper brushing my skin.
Scratchy needles pierce my skin I am a missionary in a hair shirt
Pious and devout disciple of sun, sky, earth and water

Enveloped in a eucalyptus cloud, enjoyable penance of drawing class
Portfolio in hand
Wonder, will we free form? Strokes shift with the music
Fun, intriguing, refreshing
Beyond the claustrophobic norm.

I walk into class
Instructor looks into my face
Protracted seconds of deep study, contemplation
Quince blossom face with rising bubble gum blush
"Hmm, interesting combination, your face and the plum shirt."

ജ്ഞ

The Large Blue Jar

By Judith Yarbrough

I had a terrible cold and could not sleep. I went into my mom's room and started to cry that I could not sleep and I could not breathe. She said, "Hop on the bed, get under the covers, and I will be right back with something that will help." She went into the bathroom and came back with a large blue jar. At first I looked surprised, wondering, "What in a bathroom could possibly help me sleep or help me breathe?" She opened the jar, and although the odor was strong, it had a soothing smell and I thought Mom always knows best.

She opened up my pajama top, took a small amount of this white cream on her fingers and spread it on my chest. I told my mom, "It's just like a miracle, Mom. I can breathe, and maybe if I can stay in your bed, I will be able to sleep better. Can I Mom?"

She put the lid on the jar and said, "I guess you can stay here in my bed tonight." I thought how great this blue jar was. It made me feel better, and I got to stay in Mom's bed. I immediately thought, "I hope this blue jar lasts forever."

ஐ

The Noxzema Jar Age 5

By Marilou Barsam

As a child, I was fascinated with the objects that sat on top of my grandmother's bedroom dresser. Each of them had a special place, as my grandmother was a very organized person. She used to say often, "When you use something, best thing is put back where come from." (English was a second language.)

These words, repeated multiple times in the course of my lifetime, have served as some sort of mantra to my own sense and need of order and organization.

But back to her dresser. It was made of very smooth blond wood, and its top was so shiny from the Pledge lacquering applied to it every Saturday morning, that I often imagined a miniature me ice skating on its gleaming surface.

A doily handmade by my grandmother sat squarely in the middle of the long and narrow dresser, serving as some sort of boundary for what her most special items were, sitting there so proudly in their assigned positions, nestled between the beige crocheted hooks of fine doily threads.

When my grandmother was busy cooking or watching her favorite TV shows, I would take the opportunity to sneak into her bedroom, pretending I was looking for something, when all along I had one mission—to explore these precious items calling to me like sirens of the sea: "Here, touch me; here, smell me."

One of my favorites was a fancy glass perfume bottle with a stopper on top shaped like the top of a tootsie roll pop. I would gently wiggle the head-shaped handle out of the top of the bottle and hold its graceful neck-like protrusion up against my nose.

While inhaling soft, flowery scents, I would recall images of my grandmother dressed up for special occasions and memories of everything from family reunions to fancy weddings to major holidays. Somehow the fumes from that small bottle would waft me into the past, bringing back strong images of some of the happiest times of my young life.

Next to the perfume bottle sat the prized Fuller hairbrush, its ebony, silky handle made from pure white ivory—the tusk of some exotic far away elephant that had sacrificed its horns and life to become a household item.

The soft black bristles called to me. As I ran my fingers through them, I pictured them, in turn, sliding gracefully through the salt and pepper strands of my grandmother's fine hair, many still lingering behind, woven intricately between the brush's bristles.

And then—there it was—my favorite, the midnight blue deep jewel-toned Noxzema jar, the grand holder of the creamy snow-like substance that reminded me of the marshmallow cream on my peanut butter sandwiches.

Every evening, I would stand afar in the hall, watching as my grandmother slowly dipped her fingers into the dreamy mixture, bringing two small white clouds of it up to her face and then slowly massaging her cheeks with the cream until it melted into her soft and smooth skin. Looking back at how little money my grandparents had, this ritual was probably the closest she ever got to the indulgent equivalent of a present day massage; yet somehow, evident from the smile and look of contentment on her face, this private and self-soothing routine probably served her just as well.

Later at night, when she tucked me into bed and gently kissed me goodnight, the lingering scent of the Noxzema cream would remind me of how safe I was in her presence and help me drift off to my own dreamtime world.

4

HOLIDAYS

Valentine's Day

By Bruce Nickerson

Today is February 12, and every year about this date, I get nervous about February 14. What did we do last year? Just a mutual card exchange? A yellow boxed Whitman Sampler which I gave her with a pang of guilt about the caloric denseness of those semisweet dark chocolates filled with gooey delicious sweet stuff?

Or did we go out to dinner after I bought her flowers—bright red carnations probably: Red, the color of love and passion. Carnations because they last like my love for her? Carnations because they are cheap, more like!

How did she respond?

Should I plan for this day this year? Or make it a surprise? Suppose I plan a surprise and find she has something else to do; will I get upset?

Woe is me! Supposed to be a day filled with love, but it brings me anxiety and worry. What if I go "over the top," as I frequently do, and smother her with effusive expressions of undying everlasting love that I will contradict the very next week by not doing the laundry?

I think, maybe, we just did cards last year. She is not one for external displays of emotion. An "I love you" is an outburst for her.

Now I remember—she gave me a card with a frog on the front bouncing all around and being bombarded with little hearts and ending up in the bottom right corner cockeyed and holding its head. Inside it said, "I love you so much it hurts." She signed it, "Ribbit."

Well, Saint Valentine, however you started this nonsense, you have me in a dither. Just remembered how, in elementary school, there was a big cardboard box gaudily decorated with red and white crepe paper into which we deposited our Valentines. Then, there was the worry that we would not get many and our classmates would cruelly comment on our unpopularity.

But what to do now? She is my wife after all.

For God's sake (sorry Saint Valentine), what can one expect from a day that this year follows Friday the 13th?

ഇരു

Independence Day

By Charlotte Christen

Fourth of July, Independence Day, one of the few holidays without encumbering expectations or traditions for me to uphold.

Growing up in Wisconsin, this day meant sparklers and perhaps a picnic in the backyard. In my teens, it also meant the after-dark fireworks displays at Menominee Park on the north side of town, ear-tingling rockets and fiery sprays of multicolored stars showering down in arcs into the waters of Miller's Bay on Lake Winnebago, a scene I'd attempt to duplicate with colored pencils and paper the next day, never satisfactorily.

For some people, the holiday is like a carefully patterned and pieced quilt with each square exactly alike, each holiday exactly like those in years gone by. Beautiful and comfortable in its traditional design, with a perfection I could never attain in quilting or in life.

My holiday is more like a crazy quilt displaying a myriad of unrelated experiences in locations across the country and over the ocean with the date on the July page of the calendar being the only commonality. Oddly shaped and sized pieces cut from differently textured fabrics of experience are stitched together haphazardly with a selection of decorative stitches. These squares, triangles and rectangles portray everything from listening to the Declaration of Independence presented by a descendent of John Adams at the town of Lincoln's Bicentennial celebration in 1976, to watching fireworks over Niagara Falls from the porch of a Canadian motel.

One patch is stitched in for riding on a farm wagon to go strawberry picking with my brother-in-law and our kids, and later sliding the fruit onto trays and into his new dehydrator.

Dated 1969, another piece of this crazy quilt pictures my husband, Jerry, at Epoufette, Michigan, on the upper peninsula of that state declaring his personal independence from tobacco to coincide with a move to Ann Arbor where he chose to begin teaching Air Force ROTC as a non-smoker.

Several musically embroidered patches sewn to this crazy quilt include notes for the 1812 Overture on the Esplanade in Boston, and for lawn seats at Tanglewood. These date back to when we were young enough to not mind large crowds. Will Smith is pictured on one of the pieces for the year we went to the theatre to see the movie *Independence Day* on that appropriate day of its release.

Unembellished sections are included for the times in England and Germany where, without the abundance of reminders that it was our own country's birthday, the day was overlooked.

A sun-faded square is sewn on for the holiday spent camping at John's Pond on Cape Cod, where we cooked our very first lobster, and another patch exists for a vintage picnic celebration on the green at Sturbridge Village where children rolled barrel hoops and patriotic sermons were delivered in the village meeting house.

Among the jumble on this hodgepodge Independence Day crazy quilt are numerous Fourth of July parades, mostly displaying far too many small Wisconsin towns where, with snare drum, moccasins, red-sequined headband and feather, I marched in the front row of the Oshkosh High School Girls' Drum and Bugle Corps, popular throughout the state during the summer months, more for our white-fringed short red skirts and sleeveless tops than for musical abilities.

In recent years, bits and pieces of road maps found places on the crazy quilt along with the awareness that most people had already arrived at their chosen destinations for this day and were now busily assembling their own holiday quilts, leaving the roads less crowded for those of us vacationing before or after the actual holiday.

It is a true day of independence, no special cake that has to be baked to Aunt Emily's specifications and frosted with her personal recipe for fudge icing, no particular brand of bratwurst that must be located, bought and parboiled in the precise proportions of beer, onions and spices and no parade needing to be watched because it has always been a part of the celebration. There is nothing to feel nostalgic about but life itself and its wonderful array of experiences.

Perhaps my feeling toward the day is the result of many moves creating physical distance from family members, or maybe it is a natural realization reached with age and maturity. Some might say it is a sour grapes reaction to a day without personal traditions, but my preference is to consider it as a day to be free to spend the hours as I wish, something more easily done when there are no expectations.

Now the day is past and maps of the New York and Massachusetts Turnpikes are overlaid with an embroidered design featuring a spectacular lasagna dinner with my daughter as the latest addition to my Independence Day Crazy Quilt.

ꙮ

The Fourth of July

By Katherine Picard

Towards the end of June I flip the calendar pages ahead to see what's coming up in July. The Fourth leaps off the page with promises of celebrations and fireworks as well as those who celebrate their birthdays on the holiday: Our dear friend, Walter, who died last year in his eighties, but is only a memory away; my much younger cousin, Jenny, never met, but spoken with on the phone; and, of course, Louis "Satchmo" Armstrong, who was born on the Fourth of July in 1900. I met him and his singer, Velma Middleton, when I was a young girl. He talked to my parents and me between sets and gave us his autograph on the back of a photograph my Dad had in his wallet. See, my Dad is a trumpet player, so we would go to see the big names in concert at venues in Pennsylvania.

Now, my family and I go to band concerts on the Fourth. Our daughter and her husband are musicians and the summer concert series always includes the Fourth of July. I marvel at how my daughter can stand and play the piccolo solo in "Stars and Stripes Forever" in front of the multitudes of celebrants. This year there was no concert to attend; towns had no money for fireworks and concerts. So, I watched the Boston Pops on TV—not quite the same! Besides, I hate fireworks choreographed to music!

As I glance over the days of July on the calendar, the last two weeks are sadly empty. Every year for over thirty years, when it became hot and humid here in Massachusetts, we packed the car, and Dick, Steven, Nicole and I headed north. We stayed at a camp on the Sandy River Pond seven miles from Rangeley, Maine. We discovered this magical place when we stopped at The Potter's Wheel to ask for directions to the Appalachian Trail. Frank, the potter, and his sweet wife, Mildred, greeted us warmly, gave us directions, and off we went. A year or so later, when we were looking for a vacation place, I called them up and found they had a vacancy in Number Two. Number Two had two bedrooms, a pantry/storage area, a bathroom, an open kitchen/living room with a fieldstone fireplace for heat, and a screen porch which literally overhung the water. Water for the kitchen and bathroom came from a collection pool on top of the hill across the road. It was gravity fed through thick black hoses that went under the road and snaked their way to the various camps. There was a well with a pump for drinking water, gas stove and refrigerator, but no electricity. At night there were a million stars illuminating the black sky and one time we even saw a moon bow.

It was indeed a special place. We watched the loons with their new babies, had moose and deer encounters. One afternoon a bear came tumbling down the hill, hit the side of the camp, and jumped into the lake and swam away. We could use the row boat, swim in the icy water, play board games, read, go on adventures, and, of course, hang out with Frank and Mildred. Frank was a Renaissance man, a professional trumpet player, educator, summer children's camp owner, artist, sculptor, silversmith, and potter. Their camp, Number Five, was filled with books. You always had to read what he recommended, and the heck with what you had brought to read.

Diminutive Mildred ran the show like a cruise director, taking care of her select tenants, feeding us, offering advice, loving the children and Schnapps, our Schnauzer. Eventually, she became "my other mother."

After Frank died and his ashes were scattered near the waterfall across the lake, Mildred ran the camps for a few years by herself. We ate supper together every night and our routines were not the same as when the children were little and we brought our dog. Finally, she gave the camps to her son, and even she didn't go up there anymore.

She moved to a condo in Newburyport where she once had a beauty shop as a young woman and new bride. After some time, her health declined and she moved to New Hampshire to be with her granddaughter, Monique, and her family. She had raised Monique and her sister, Loren, and they were always at the camps, too. We saw Mildred last August to celebrate her eighty-ninth birthday, and sadly "my other mother" died shortly after in September.

Piles of dirt have been bulldozed to seal the road entering the camps, and the more hidden road is chained off when no one is there. Dick and I have walked through the woods and visited the camp site, but the fizzle has faded from the magic. The energy has changed and though the natural setting is still as lovely, the ambience is no longer special.

Every year at the beginning of July we are drawn to go to Maine. We have since stayed at other camps and we have rented by the week, but it is never the same. How could it be!

ꙮ

Christmas/Bart the Bartender

By Lisa R. Benson

Christmas is right around the corner and I don't want to go back to Maryland to celebrate. I think this year I'll have to make up an excuse to stay in Philly. Won't get too many customers at the bar on Christmas Eve, but it'll be better than explaining that, yes, I'm still single, and, yes, I'm still a bartender. Moreover, of course I'm proud of my younger brother's baseball scholarship and that my older brother passed the Bar exam to be a lawyer. The only bar exam I ever passed was mixing cocktails and even that's a disaster once *she* walks into the bar. She really messes with my concentration…

Where was I? Right! Maryland. So I think I'll say I can't make it this year. Sorry, Mom, the car broke down again.

Yeah, I'll call Christmas Eve. I'll say I've been working on it all morning and I can't get it running. The mechanics are all closed now. No, I don't need Dad to get on the phone and walk me through it. The only problem is pretending like I'm coming before Christmas Eve, and sitting through phone calls of excited plans and dodging questions about when I'll be coming.

If I can manage the deception, Mom will be disappointed, but there'll be nothing she can do about it. Besides, she'll have her two perfect sons with her that day. What does she need Bart the bartender for?

ཉ

Christmas/I am Charlie!

By Kathleen Shure

Christmas is right around the corner and I know what I always do! Finish up sweeping the street and sidewalk and emptying the public trash bins. Then I like to walk home. I know everybody on the way home. They say, "Hi Charlie!" and I say "Hi!" back.

I miss my mother.

I think I am fifty-two, that's what Joe next door tells me, but I don't know. I know I like Pop Tarts and Pepsi for breakfast, especially on Christmas.

I wish Dad was here to get a tree, but the room I live in on Main Street is too small for one anyway.

I like to take my tongue and feel the spaces between my teeth— it feels good and makes me smile at everyone as I walk down the street in my blue pants and jacket. I like my blue pants and jacket. Joe says I should get new ones for Christmas because these are "old." I don't know what he means.

I like to watch TV all night on the couch, and for Christmas I will do that more!

5

ADVENTURE

The Shadow Across the Moon

By Linda Christen

You know when you see something so often that you just no longer see it? It melts into the palate of your day; maybe somewhere in the unthought-of corners of your mind you know it's there, you trust and rely on its being there, but seldom think about it. Like the shadow across the moon. When was the last time Leah had actually paused in the night and looked, studied, focused upon that shadow? Yet she always knew it was there. Like her Great-Great-Grandma Helene's watch hanging around her neck, softly ticking the moments of her life, only to be heard if it were to stop. Some things in life are like that. You don't have to look, you can just trust. Like leaning against that old brick wall at the side of the playground when she was a kid. It was there; it supported her and cooled her in its shade. She didn't have to see it before leaning back.

This was nothing like that. Tonight was pitch black, and when she did look up into the thick velvet of sky toward the comforting silver beacon, she jumped. Never a gutsy one, seeing the moon without its shadow had to be a harbinger of something.

What else was amiss? She ran as the crow flies; slashing her way through the wheat field looking for Jimmy, she just kept telling herself it was nothing. So what if the shadow was gone? It shouldn't have the force to upset her so entirely. When she found Jimmy, he'd talk sense into her. He was always the calm, clearheaded one. No bats in the belfry there! Not like her, always imagining things not there and not seeing what was.

At the edge of the field, she just had to head up the street to the house. Leah could see it clear as day, with the full shadowless moon guiding her way. Finally at the door, banging for entry, it opened and she went in. She'd been here a million times, practically grew up here, but never had it been so frigid. Why didn't anyone stoke the fire? Loud voices from the back, maybe they would know what was going on.

She felt her way along the familiar old corridor, gently brushing against the soft wallpaper which she knew had lovely old flocked peachy roses vining their way from the intricately carved ancient oak baseboard all the way up to its foot-wide ornate partner molding at the ceiling. After the next doorway, at the end of the hall was the kitchen—that's where the voices were. Darker than the night, but she knew this home, these halls and rooms, the oak and rose wall paper, she knew them as well as she knew herself. They had been a part of her life since before her memory. But for the cold and darkness, this home was her constant.

Then she heard it, screaming for her attention—silence. Great-Great-Grandma Helene's watch hung still around her neck, but with no comforting tick.

Feeling her way past the door frame, there was the hard cut-glass doorknob followed by the soft, warm oak door frame. What was that brushing against her face? Was it a cob web, everywhere cob webs? In all her life there had never been a spider in this house. Leah's namesake, her dearly loved short-as-she-was-wide Auntie Tilley was far too fastidious and loved her home too much to allow for a spider web.

Odd they get thicker, on her face; she has to brush them off.

Suddenly, cool hands on her neck, a crisp voice in her ear.

Where had he come from? All the noise was ahead, in the kitchen; she could see the light under the door.

Deep sharp words at her ear, "Hold still!"

Leah's final misty thought, as she slunk through the spider webs to the dusty floor: "Why was there no shadow on the moon?...."

ꟾ

The Old Barn

By Bob Beckwith

Turn right onto Plantation Road, drive one mile, take the left fork onto the dirt road, go a mile and a half until you see the foundation and some rotted timbers of the old barn. Park your car, and using a flashlight, walk to the back of the barn where you will find a small bungalow, enter it—sit in the chair pulled up to the table and flash your light three times out the side window, I will enter with your grandfather's watch.

Call me crazy, stupid, or even a daredevil, but I'm doing this tonight. My granddaddy was a high profile trial lawyer, well known throughout the state of Alabama as was my father and now yours truly. We've all taken on some pretty controversial cases—many involving landowners against their black help. My granddaddy instilled in all of us that if we see injustice, do all you can to make it right—regardless of the color of a person's skin.

Being a traditional southern family, we cherish our heritage and our possessions. Our law firm has even occupied the same space for three generations.

Tonight I'm on a mission to retrieve my granddaddy's pocket watch. It was stolen after a highly publicized case he fought and lost. His client, a black farmhand, was accused of setting a fire that destroyed his master's farmhouse and barn. My grandfather knew his client was innocent, however, the jury, all white as always, would not consider all the evidence. After the trial, the family thought my grandfather deliberately blew the case which sent his client to jail for thirty-five years. Nothing could be further from the truth; however, try telling that to the black population who were used to getting screwed more times than not in court.

About six months after the trial, my granddaddy's pocket watch mysteriously disappeared, never to be seen again. That watch was his pride and joy. Given to him by his father upon graduation from The University of Alabama School of Law. It was handsomely monogrammed, encased in highly polished gold, with a three-carat pear-shaped ruby dangling from the end of the watch chain. The letter described the Rockford pocket watch perfectly—even down to the worn spot on the front cover, a spot made by granddaddy's left thumb as he would caress his watch while pondering a case.

It's eight p.m., the time the letter told me to start out from my office for the designated meeting spot. No one knows what I am up to tonight. All I told my family was that I had a meeting that would probably run quite late.

Ok, I'm on the dirt road. Good thing I brought the Jeep, by the look of the rocks and ruts, this path is not too heavily travelled. Bumpity—bump—bump—clunk, ah that must be the old barn just ahead. Something's real strange here—I mean not that this whole escapade isn't strange enough, but there's no other car around. Oh well—too late to turn back now. Got my flashlight on; now to maneuver through this heavy underbrush and bittersweet vines—damn, I should have brought a brighter flashlight—what's that moving? Oh man, I've just walked into a coyote den. Stop—step back slowly—slower—slower—don't make any quick moves. Ok, ok—good—I think. Where's a stick—gotta find a stick quick—that'll give me some protection in case an animal decides to charge in order to protect his territory. Ah, got one. Not too swift of me, out here in this wild vegetation in my Armani three-piece suit. Ouch—what was that? Thorns! Where the hell's the path—the letter said there'd be a path to follow. Smhh—smhh— there's a skunk around here. Oh good, at least I found the path.

Ok, around the large cellar hole—yeah, this must be the place—it's an old farmhand's bungalow—looks like it hasn't been lived in for decades. Up the front steps—crack, dammit, my foot almost broke through the stair. Quick, grab the railing; it's no help—it's rotten too. Ok, up to the next step, ah that's better. Turn the doorknob and push. Creeeek—what's that?! Oh my God, three rats are staring at my light—man their red eyes are big. Quick, hit the floor with my stick. That did it—off they go through the hole in the wall next to the cobwebbed netted fireplace…

Oh man, what am I doing here? Yeah, good trial lawyers are willing to take chances to win cases, but this is just being stupid. Besides coping with all these wild animals, I don't even know who the hell I'm meeting here—or if it's legit. Granddaddy, I sure hope you appreciate all the chances I'm taking to get your watch back. Lord, if I get out of this without getting bitten, stabbed, shot or strangled, I promise I'll never play superhero again.

No sense getting all shook up now, too late for that, and besides, whoever is behind this asinine scheme has probably been watching my every move since I got out of the car.

There's the chair by the table—walk slowly—careful--the floor's probably weak. Careful—careful—test each step. Ah, I made it—I'm in the chair—flutter, flutter, flutter—why not—might as well add a couple of bats winging around the room. Blink—blink—blink, that dusty portrait on the wall—did he just blink at me when I shined my light that way? Stay cool—stay cool, at least that's what they taught us in law school. Never let them see you sweat. Right now I'm not so worried about sweating—I'm more worried about what I might do in my pants.

Ok, the moment of truth, I just flashed my light three times out the side window. Wham! Holy shit—what was that? Clomp, clomp, clomp. From the side door enters a large, well-built black man. He's got to be almost seven feet, and look at those giant hands. He puts his hand firmly on my shoulder and says, "Jonathan Eldridge Williams the third, Esquire—I'm Billy Parkhurst—does that last name ring a bell counselor?"

Parkhurst—Parkhurst, oh great he's a relative. Johnnie Parkhurst was the black farmhand my granddaddy couldn't acquit of the fire.

"Yes, I recognize the name. Your family never forgave my grandfather for losing that case." All that's going through my head now is, you ass, Jonathan, you've been had. This is big time payback—Parkhurst style.

"You're right, Jonathan, my family never did forgive your granddaddy for that case. They knew all along it was a white cover up simply to convict another black man for something he never did. And yes, it was my people who stole your granddaddy's cherished pocket watch in retaliation. However, I've researched this case fully and have come to the conclusion that your grandfather did all he could to make it a fair trial and get an acquittal for Johnnie. And I know you and your daddy have taken on many, many cases involving black people over the years—a lot of them for gratis. I also know your granddaddy established an endowment to help educate the children of black incarcerated victims—and your family has always done these things very quietly. Attorney Williams, you're sitting in Johnnie's house right now. And the cellar you walked by is all that remains of the barn my granddaddy was accused of burning down. My brother and I own all this land now, including another eighteen hundred acres to the right of the hot-topped road you first came down. We are soy bean farmers, plus we own a computer software company, all because of your family. You see my daddy was able to go to college and become a doctor, thanks to your family's endowment. This opportunity allowed him to earn a good living—good enough that my brother and I were able to graduate from Duke University. I keep this decrepit old house to remind me that all is not perfect between black and whites; however, things are improving—enough so that we have become fairly wealthy. Therefore, as promised counselor, here is your granddaddy's beloved pocket watch, as well as a check for two million dollars for your family's educational endowment fund."

"Billy—I don't know what to say." Fingering the warn spot in the watch, I continue. "I feel like granddaddy is here—with us—right now—accepting your most generous gift—but more than that he is smiling—knowing that all his hard work and public criticism was not in vain."

"Counselor, will you join me in my real home for an evening drink? You surely deserve it, after proving once again, that you and your family will go to all extremes to accomplish your purpose."

"Billy, a little Jack Daniels on the rocks will taste real good right now."

"Follow me counselor."

ജ്ര

Room 435

By Charlotte Christen

Sarah would have to "sleep fast" as her grandmother used to say. The dinner meeting with her new client lasted too long and it was now past eleven o'clock. As she drove through Poughkeepsie's dark streets, carefully following the GPS directions to her hotel, she decided she liked what she'd seen of this town so far. She was told that a couple of decades ago it went through a period of urban decay but managed to revitalize itself. It had spirit and Sarah liked that.

She found the hotel easily and when she picked up her key, despite the late hour the desk staff was cheerful. Pulling her luggage into the elevator, she simultaneously pushed the button for the fourth floor. Room 435 was not far down the hall; she slid the card in and out of the lock while pushing the door open. Time to sleep.

This job was becoming burdensome, the continual driving from client to client, giving lectures and instructions; it was wearing. Sarah needed to do a lot of studying to keep up with new developments and she was frequently tired. It was exciting when she was younger—traveling, dinners out in fancy restaurants, new people and an occasional affair, though never a serious relationship. Her lifestyle left little time for just "chilling out" with her few friends. She had many associates at her firm and was superficially friendly with them in a way, but that's how it needed to remain, superficial. If a downsizing occurred, these work friends were her competitors for the remaining employment slots after the bloodletting, not a safe group to be "chilling out" with. The salary, Sarah admitted, her consultant's salary, was definitely a perk, as was the freedom. Still, Sarah was tired; tired and lonely.

She changed into her pajamas and tumbled into bed, asleep in seconds. Sometime during the night, she became aware of a warm overall presence nestled beside her in the bed. It startled her. How could another person get into her room? She was about to scream when a soothing male voice said, "The hotel was filled so they asked at the desk if I minded sharing a room. I won't hurt you. You don't mind, do you? I'll leave early in the morning."

The comforting nearness of this other body, and her deep fatigue, overpowered Sarah's fears, and she drifted back to sleep.

True to his word, he did not hurt her and by the time she was fully awake in the morning, he was gone. There was a note on the desk thanking her for being kind enough to allow him to stay. It was not signed.

How could a hotel of this stature allow something like this to happen? Her company booked only at the safest hotels, or so she thought. Sarah planned to complain at the desk before leaving, to demand explanations and apologies. She was lucky to be alive.

Yet, when Sarah left the hotel, she dropped the key card at the desk without a word. Despite the night's disturbance, she felt fine, and she drove off refreshed and alert, ready for her next assignment at another town in New York's Washington Irving Country, home of Ichabod Crane and Rip Van Winkle, stories she loved when she read them in high school. She actually knew someone, a family friend, who was a descendant of one of the Van Tassels portrayed in the "Legend of Sleepy Hollow." The woman's portrait hung on their living room wall. Driving the winding roads from Poughkeepsie to New Paltz, Sarah pictured Rip tossing bowling balls at Nine Pins with the bearded ghosts from Henry Hudson's crew out there in the distant Catskill Mountains.

Two weeks later, when it was time for Sarah to return to Poughkeepsie, she'd considered changing hotels; after all, it had been irresponsible of them to double book her room. No matter how busy, it was wrong. Implausibly though, when the time came, she'd asked the travel agent at work to request this same hotel and room. So after a day's work and dinner, she found herself unlocking the door to room 435.

Sarah readied herself for bed, propped up the bed pillows and settled in to read. She read only a chapter of her book before snuggling down under the comforter to sleep. In a short while she became once again aware of a warm body curled up to her with an arm thrown protectively over her shoulder. Was she dreaming? Was she awake? What was she thinking when she decided to come back to this hotel, to this room? Still, Sarah felt safe. He spoke, "We seem to be on the same travel schedule and staying at a very busy hotel. Don't mind me, I'll be leaving early." The note in the morning said, "Have a good meeting and a safe trip." Again, no name.

Every time Sarah came through Poughkeepsie, she had the same experience. Sometimes Sarah and her mystery guest talked about books or movies before she fell asleep. It was like having a real friend to relax with, and she began to depend on her follow-up appointments with the Poughkeepsie client that brought her to this hotel and nights in room 435. She felt more grounded, less dissatisfied with some of the more tedious aspects of her job. Her renewed attitude carried over to negotiations with other clients as well, and she found herself even more successful than before. Once more, Sarah loved her job.

As work with the Poughkeepsie client neared its end, Sarah began to worry about not being able to return to room 435. She'd become dependent upon the comforting presence of her fellow traveler. She knew little of his personal life, but then he knew little of hers. Theirs was a comforting detached-yet-close friendship; one asking nothing of the other than to have a time of peaceful sharing and support. She knew about his reading and movie preferences, or did she? It was Sarah doing most of the talking on those nights. She admitted to herself that her mysterious friend mainly listened.

On her final visit, Sarah was restless and agitated throughout the celebratory banquet. She accepted the company's thanks for her dedicated and expert consultation and the extensive work she had done with their company. It had been another long day and she was eager to get to the hotel. But now her schedule changed. She'd been texted during the dessert; she would not be staying here tonight and she needed to drive to Albany for an early morning meeting with a new client. The drive would take several hours, so she called ahead to request a late arrival. Sarah collected her luggage from the hotel and whispered a reluctant goodbye to room 435. Leaving Poughkeepsie, Sarah headed west to New Paltz and then north on 87 to Albany. More Irving country.

Checking into the hotel, she was startled to see her room number: It was 435. What a coincidence. Sarah wasted little time before settling her head down into the feather pillow. As she dropped off to sleep, she heard a familiar comforting voice, "Hi! It's me. I thought you might need some company after that long drive. I'll leave early so I won't be in your way in the morning. Goodnight, Sarah. Sleep peacefully."

ᘓᘐ

A Flying Adventure

By Katherine Picard

The flight attendants continued to run through the crash-landing drill with the passengers. Their ashen faces and terrified eyes conveyed that this was the real deal and not a drill. We were on our way to Margarita Island for a winter respite and had left the mainland of Venezuela behind us.

As we were approaching the island and getting ready to land, the pilot realized that the landing gear was locked in place. He circled for an eternity while trying all of his tricks to get the wheels to drop while the attendants prepared us for the "belly" landing that was to take place. At long last, the pilot announced the landing gear had released and he was going to be able to land somewhat normally.

We touched down and I caught a glimpse of the emergency equipment that was waiting for us in case the emergency landing had occurred. There was one lonely, antiquated fire engine and one aged rescue truck! It was then that I was really alarmed at what might have been!

As an after note, we found out later that this plane had mechanical problems on several flights before and after our flight. It was finally taken out of service—none too soon!

ꕤ

Charlie on Main St.

By Kathleen Shure

I was just walking down Main St. as usual on my way home, JUST WALKING HOME, OK?! See, he comes up to me and grabs my broom and pan and throws them over the fence into someone's yard and laughs like this:

HA, HA CHARLIE!

"Look Joey," I says, "GO AWAY! AWAY!"

He just gets closer, up to my face and laughs: AHA –AH!

I yell back, "AWAY, AWAY!" I try to climb the fence, but he holds onto my pants. I am cold and crying. All I want to do is get my broom and pan and go home to my TV and make a bowl of Campbell's soup.

I make a face at him and stand there. I wait, wait.

Joey waits. And makes a face, too.

A kid on a bike comes by, and old lady walks by with her grocery bags.

I wait, I spit on the ground.

Joey laughs, and spits on the ground.

Joey says he has to go pee, and has no more time for nonsense, and he leaves.

I climb over the fence, get my broom and dust pan, and walk home, where Joey is NOT.

ꕥ

6

HUMOR

Even though many stories in this book are funny, these are presented here because they best represent a category of laugh-out-loud stories.

The Wake

By E.M. Karrick

Nobody likes to talk about death. We all know it will happen one day but that's all we know about it for sure… with some exceptions. The Catholics, for instance: They have a clear idea of the hereafter and live their lives hoping they've done a good enough job for it to be a heavenly one. And the Irish Catholics actually seem to enjoy a death. They celebrate it with a loud drunken party called a Wake.

"Can ya getta pint in heaven Father?" chortled Seamus, a cherry snouted octogenarian, as he raised his own and lurched forward, falling into Father who, in turn, fell backwards into the big bosomed lady standing behind him whose husband was hosting the affair from a red mahogany casket at the far end of the room. Thrown off balance, she in turn fell backwards and the three of them went down like big lead dominos, making loud successive thuds as they hit the floor. The widow's skirt ended up at her waist, exposing her corpulent underparts and the complex underpinnings she'd worn to conceal them.

"Oh my Lord, Gerty!" shouted her thin-lipped sister, putting her hands to her face as the crowd broke into gales of laughter.

The trio lay in a great undignified heap on the ground, not quite knowing whose arms and legs were whose as a gaggle of giggling children looked on wide-eyed but were promptly whisked away by their horrified but also giggling mothers. Father untangled himself first, sitting up, trying unsuccessfully to pull Gerty's untowardly positioned skirt down to a place of modesty. "Father," she slurred loudly, "I've always fancied you. Shall we have a go at it?"

Father's face turned ten shades of scarlet as he grasped her arm and tried to lift her to sitting. Up she came like a giant sea whale from the deep, snorts and all, seated now, legs spread wide apart, fully exposing her privates. "Fer the love a God!" gasped her thin-lipped sister, her face now beet red. "Yer showin' everythin' He's given ya!"

But Gerty was unfazed. Father stumbled his way to standing, reached down, grabbed her arms and with all his might, pulled her up off the floor. The pint-toasting octogenarian who'd started it all followed soon after, standing beside Father and the besotted widow who was weaving unsteadily back and forth, looking like she might just begin the unholy tumble all over again.

The crowd gave them an ear splitting round of applause. "Fer sure ya woke the dead with that one" shouted a glassy eyed gent who was standing next to the coffined host—Gerty's dear departed Finney, whom she'd dressed in his cherished Saint Patty's Day best: a Kelly green leprechaun outfit, complete with silver buttons, feathered cap and pointy-toed shoes. They'd fixed an impish grin on his face and his hands were clasping a large bouquet of plastic four leaf clovers. Standing next to the glassy eyed gent, peering into the coffin, was a quiet, shy, velvet-frocked little girl. It was her first time at a wake. Frowning slightly, she looked up at him and whispered: "Is that how you have to dress when you go to heaven?"

ꕥ

Class Cancelled Prompt

By Bruce Nickerson

(The entire first paragraph was a prompt.)

I turned my Toyota into the driveway of the historic building for my writing class but instantly noticed something must be wrong. All the lights were out, the building abandoned like a school at Christmastime. In the dark, I reached across to the passenger seat and dug one hand into my purse until I could feel my calendar. I pulled out the tiny leather keeper-of-my-life, its once hard binder now worn from a year's worth of abuse. It was clearly time for the 2009 clone. I flipped on the dome light and hastily turned to December, flipping the pages best I could despite my thick leather gloves. Hmmm, right there in black ink it said class was scheduled, so I shut the car and worked my way to the door in the dark while wondering if my desire to write was worth all this hassle? I managed to find the door in the dark and pulled at the handle. Nothing; jammed shut. The only thing I could see was my breath creating steam. Ah, a cup of hot tea would be nice, but noooo, I was out there in the cold, ice forming in my nostrils. Was it even safe standing there in darkness? How was Bedford's crime rate anyway? Just to be sure, I pushed my coat sleeve back and pressed the stem on my watch to light it up and double check the time: yup, six-thirty, the teacher and rest of the class surely should be here by now. I thought I'd just wait a bit more in the car, and started to walk when I suddenly recalled a *second* memo from the teacher saying, what was it?, oh shit, that's right, she had made an error and there was no class on December 11! It was meant to be December 18!

And I bothered to dress carefully for nothing! Well, at least I had a few hours free for myself this evening. I walked over the parking area black ice, skidding a few times before reaching the side of the car. My glove-covered fingers fumbled awkwardly for keys in the Land's End bag I carried, finally retrieving them and jamming what I hoped was the right one in the direction of the car lock. It slid into the hole. I opened the door, got in, my mind racing feverishly and excitedly at the prospect of a few hours all my own. I tried to remember where it was—the Escadrille? Or was it in Lawrence? Methuen? Dracut? Over the border in Pelham? Damn! Maybe further west out near 495? My hands shook as I tore open the glove compartment, grabbed at my makeup kit, ripped it open and, with the help of a dim dome light and the rear view mirror, started applying my lipstick, eye shadow, darkening my eyebrows—the regular routine—hoping I could find that drag bar before I had to be home.

ꟊ

The Color of Love

By Mindy Pollack-Fusi

I started the day smiling. You walked in with four quarts of paint—crimson, violet, turquoise and bright yellow—and I imagined a day filled with vibrant colors stroked onto the walls of our new apartment. We'd paint messily all day long until we'd laugh ourselves silly into our glass-enclosed shower and melt away the smeared colors clinging to our tired flesh. Afterward, we'd relax with a martini or two.

But, no! You had to get that cellphone call in the middle of the turquoise bedroom trim. There we were, standing atop the two tall wooden chairs, stretching up to dab the paint onto the trim, when "I Caught Santa Kissing Mommy" chimed from your pants' pocket.

"Damn! My cellphone!" you shouted while attempting to put down the paint pan without dripping onto our new hardwood floors or spilling the turquoise on your jeans, already covered with crimson splotches that looked as though you'd cut yourself and bled through.

You moved toward the hallway and dug out your phone, turning a shade of white I can't quite describe. Maybe eggshell or bone, or maybe one of those Pottery Barn colors like "My Old Girlfriend's on the Cellphone but My New Girlfriend is Right Here with me; Now What the Hell Do I Do?"

Do you know that color, honey?

All I know is that the minute I saw the color of your face, no, the minute I heard you say "Hi" in that soft sweet voice you've always reserved for her—never for me—I knew that painting this apartment not only wasn't fun anymore, it didn't matter.

It was over. We were over.

"I hate you!" I yelled, heading for the front door, but not before dipping one foot into the quart of bright yellow and another into the violet, and taking a quick spin around our luscious little love nest.

ꕥ

Kindergarten

By E.M. Karrick

At the end of my first creative writing session, my teacher, Mindy, gave me a prompt. "A prompt," she explained, "is a word or group of words used to trigger your creative mind to open and go wherever it wants to go. Don't censor, don't edit. Don't listen to that voice in your head that tells you what you're writing is terrible and no one would want to read it. Some will like it, some won't–in the same way we don't all like the same authors, read the same books. It's about being you and telling your story, writing from that place. Before you start," she added, "at the top of the page, I want you to write: see, hear, taste, touch, smell." Then she gave me my prompt: Kindergarten....

KINDERGARTEN! UGH! My mind and heart went thud as I tumbled back into that dreary cavernous classroom with its too high ceilings and smells of damp, dirty dust. The room was filled with long low tables, covered with paper and crayons and.... little jars of creamy white library paste. Julie Parker used to eat it. On the lids of those jars was a little white stick that stuck straight up and looked like a very short Popsicle stick. You had to hold that stick when you pasted. Maybe that's why Julie ate it. The teachers told her not to but she did it anyway, always blushing and looking ashamed when she got caught. I liked Julie Parker. She was soft spoken, gentle and kind but her eating that paste worried me. It made me think something was wrong with her but I didn't know what. Rosy cheeked and chubby, she had long silky blond hair that made her look like an angel. I thought she might be one, except for the paste eating. I didn't think angels did that.

All day long we wore painting smocks, whether or not we painted. Made no sense to me but uncharacteristically, I didn't ask why–

probably because I loved my smock. It was sky blue with big shiny buttons and huge deep pockets. I loved looking down at that sky blue color and feeling the slippery smoothness of those big shiny buttons. But, putting my hands in its huge deep pockets was what I loved the most. The perfect place to twiddle my fingers and let my hands dance–unnoticed, unrestrained. I hated confinement of any kind and Kindergarten was nothing but. You were told to sit, more than I could bear but hidden in the pockets of my sky blue smock was my private island of freedom, at least for one part of me.

The classroom windows were nearly ceiling high and creepy, covered with a sticky haze that must have been that damp dirty dust I was always smelling. It made the trees outside blur and dimmed the sun when it tried to shine through.

I don't remember much else about that jail except the walk to and from it – the direction I much preferred. I lived a block away. A city block. I lived in Washington D.C. The walk to it was a long uphill climb on big sandy brown sidewalk squares that made thin cracks where they met. I'd hopscotch over those cracks but sometimes purposefully land on them with exuberant, defiant force. I could never quite decide if doing that was a good or a bad thing but mostly I thought it was probably bad–that someday something bad would happen to me because I'd done it. I hadn't yet heard the rhyme: "Step on a crack, break your mother's back," so that wasn't what gave me that feeling. It just felt that way. All by itself. I hated climbing that hill, hated climbing hills period. Still do to this day. When you climb a hill, you can't just relax and enjoy yourself along the way 'cause you're always doing that climbing and wanting to get to the top.

Every day, my Governess Carola would walk me to and from that jail, holding my hand to soften the pain, making me feel forever safe. I loved her so much I wanted to be her when I grew up. She was Swedish and had an accent that gave her voice an up and down lilting that made it sound like she was singing. Her soft brown hair was fixed in two long braids, coiled into perfect plump circles and pinned to either side of her head. I knew I was going to wear my hair exactly like that when I grew up. I thought about it every night before I fell asleep and knew that someday, when I was old enough and my hair was long enough, she'd show me just how to do it.

At the top of the hill was a convent. You couldn't see it though. You could only see the sky high walls surrounding it. Brick walls, covered with always green ivy cascading down the sides. My mother explained that a convent was a house where nuns lived and that they seldom left their house, didn't mix much with the rest of the world. She said nuns were holy women called sisters and the ones who lived in that particular convent were Belgian. She didn't explain the Belgian. She said holy sisters devoted their lives to God and Jesus and prayed all day long and some took a vow of silence that meant they never talked ever - for their whole lives. I knew I never wanted to be a nun.

On rare occasions, when the Holy Belgian Sisters did come out to mix with the rest of the world, I was awestruck. They wore long blue flowing robes that reached right down to the ground, making them look like they had no feet. I wondered. Their heads were adorned with big white hats whose brims stuck way out on the sides like giant bird wings. The Holy Belgian Sisters never spoke to us, only nodded, smiled and glided silently bye as if their feet, if they had any, didn't touch the ground. I never saw a door in those sky high walls so I don't know how they went in and came out. Whenever we saw them, it seemed they'd appeared out of nowhere, to mix with the rest of the world and glide.

Across the street from the Holy Belgian Sisters was Doc's Drugstore. Doc's was my favorite place to go for treats and Carola would take me there often. We'd sit at a long smooth counter on very high stools that spun you around fast when you pushed your hand hard against it and swung your legs a certain way. Under the counter were bumps of already chewed gum that Carola said naughty children had stuck there. I wished they hadn't 'cause it felt icky when I'd forget and touch them. I loved the high up of those spinning stools and Carola would always let me spin while I waited for my cherry Coke. I always ordered cherry Coke. Dark red and sweet, it was poured over a mound of finely crushed ice, set in a white paper cup held by what looked like a dulled silver goblet. It came with a straw and Carola would let me make noise with it at the end – that noise it makes when there's almost nothing left to drink. My mother never let me do that. "STOP THAT RACKET THIS INSTANT!" she'd say. "PUT THAT STRAW DOWN NOW!" Luckily, my mother was rarely the one to take me to Doc's. She was too busy at home—arranging flowers for the tables, playing her cello and telling the servants what to do.

My jail was two houses down from Doc's and it was ugly. A five-story high, sad brown stony structure with rusty black fire escapes that snaked up the sides. I can't remember the entrance but I know there must have been one. It was so unfriendly though, it not having an entrance would have seemed fitting and would have spared me the horror of those kindergarten days.

Going home was my favorite part of the day and Carola was always there to pick me up. Except once. The day I walked home alone. Looking both ways to be sure no cars were coming, I crossed the street, jumping onto the sidewalk when I reached the other side. I skipped and danced all the way down the hill, running my hand against the wrought iron fences I passed along the way. I loved the feel of that soft even bumping and the muffled sound it made. Bursting with pride that I'd made the journey home all by myself, I climbed the high steps to my front door, reached up and rang the bell. A moment later, my mother opened the door. Seeing I was alone, she looked at me wild eyed and screeched. Exactly what she screeched I can't recall, but I know it went something like this: "GET IN THE HOUSE THIS MINUTE LISA! WHAT IN GOD'S NAME (his name came up a lot in her screechings) ARE YOU DOING HERE ALONE? WHERE IS CAROLA? HAVE YOU NO SENSE? YOU COULD HAVE BEEN KIDNAPPED OR RUN OVER BY A CAR. DEAD OR WORSE!"

"Worse?" I remember thinking. Dead sounded like the very worst thing of all, what little I knew of it at that young age: In Sunday school, we had a statue of Jesus on the wall, hanging from a cross, bleeding all over the place. They told us he'd died but came alive again. "He rose from the dead," they said, and flew up to a beautiful place called heaven where he wasn't dead anymore. They said if we were good, when we died, we'd do the same thing. Heaven and the flying sounded fun, but I didn't like all the bleeding that came first, and I wasn't always good.

When my mother finished her screeching, she ended with what she always did at the end of a screeching: "DO YOU UNDERSTAND ME, LISA?" And I did understand. My ears hurt from the understanding. I tried to explain that I knew how to walk home from school by myself, that I'd looked both ways before crossing the street to be sure no cars were coming and I could run very fast so no kidnapper could ever catch me. I wanted to end with: "DO YOU UNDERSTAND ME MOTHER?" but I didn't. Instead, my heart sank, knowing no matter what I said I wouldn't be believed because I was four. And when you're four, no one thinks you know or can do anything.

I don't remember why Carola wasn't there to pick me up that day but I imagine my mother must have had quite the go 'round with her about it. She didn't get fired though, so she must have had a good excuse. Or, maybe I'd slipped out the schoolhouse door before school was actually over. Hating it as I did, that's entirely possible.

ꟷ

I Thought I Smelled a Skunk

By Katherine Picard

The passengers snaked their way down the aisles of the aircraft, comparing the tickets in their hands with the seat numbers posted overhead on the storage bins. The queue shortened as one-by-one seats were located and luggage was stowed overhead. At last I found a seat that matched the number on my ticket, stowed my gear, and settled in for the long cross-Atlantic flight back to Boston.

Scanning my fellow passengers, their diversity struck me. Old, middle-aged, young adults, teenagers, children. Some going home after a vacation in Germany; some starting their vacations in the USA; business persons, families, friends, solitary travelers. We filled the plane to capacity.

To my right was a young German man with stuffed animals in the form of snakes wrapped around the handles of his carry-on bag. Then, magician-like, he started to pull multiple bags from a shopping bag he had carried on. The bags were all filled with food—primarily treats. He said his mother and aunt packed them for him so he'd have enough to eat. He generously shared his treasures of licorice, chocolates, and cookies with those of us around him, including the crew. Fortunately, we were sitting in the front row of the plane so there was additional legroom for him to stash his collection of goody bags. He was very upbeat, going to America to visit friends, and he certainly was an entertaining travel companion.

After we were airborne, and some time had elapsed, a faint, somewhat familiar odor, settled over us. Unidentifiable as first, it became more familiar. *Skunk?* What?! We were at 35,000 feet. No animals roaming around up here. Puzzled, I looked around at the passengers, searching for the source in their open bags and possessions. Three seats on my right, I found it—the skunk smell. A young guy had taken off his sneakers and was enjoying the comfort of sitting with just his white socks on—his white socks, airing out, while their damp, skunk-like aroma wrapped around us.

Sighing, I raised my eyebrows, turned my body and head to the other direction, and tried not to breathe deeply. Is it possible to hold your breath across the entire Atlantic Ocean? I may find out.

ᘓᘐ

Ellen Tries A New Salon

By Lea Ann Knight

Pushing her hair behind her ears, Ellen stepped into the upscale salon. She wondered if this would finally be the one. The young girl at the modern Lucite desk looked up expectantly. "May I help you?"

"I'm here for a three o'clock appointment with Rebecca."

"Hmmm, let me see. Are you Ellen Goodbye? "

"Sort of. It's actually Goodby, like 'good bee.'"

She smiled blankly at me. "One moment."

The raven-haired (was that her real color?) sweet young thing, as Harry would have called her, spoke into an itsy bitsy microphone attached to her ear. "Rebecca, Mrs. Goodbye is here for her three o'clock appointment."

Oh well… She had had such high hopes for this salon. The sign on the awning outside had seemed so chic, so "with it." And in her favorite color, too. Perhaps they were "in between" receptionists.

Determined to keep an open mind, Ellen looked around and found a matching Lucite bench where she could sit and wait for the stylist that had been recommended by Linda, her tennis partner. Linda always had beautifully coiffed hair. Did she visit Rebecca every week, Ellen wondered? Surely not; didn't weekly visits to the salon go out with the free hair movement of the sixties? She could remember her grandmother Ruby walking down to the beauty parlor every Tuesday to get her hair done. Even then, the only women under the hair dryers were old and sporting thinning, blue curls. Oooh, Ellen shuddered. Some things had improved in the world of hair, even if she couldn't seem to find a reliable stylist.

Continuing to wait for Rebecca, she began to look around. It seemed Lucite was the au courant material for trendy hair salons these days. It must be a bitch to keep clean. And didn't Lucite scratch easily? Did it yellow over time? And who in the world thought sitting on Lucite would be comfortable?

Five more minutes went by. Just as she got up to complain to the empty-headed receptionist, a woman silently appeared at her elbow. Yikes! Where did she come from? Lucite doesn't provide a lot of hiding space, but somehow this woman was here, by her side, uncomfortably close. And her hair.... Oh my! Piles and piles of blond hair, teased to the ceiling, stared Ellen in the face. Oh dear. "Please don't let this be Rebecca, please don't let this be Rebecca," Ellen silently prayed.

"Hello, Mrs. Goodbye, I am Rebecca. Please follow me...."

Shoulders slumped, with an air of defeat, Ellen shuffled after the tower of hair. Best to just get this over with and start researching new salons.

ꙮ

Peas

By Lisa R. Benson

I saw him walking toward me at the dinner table, each step like an angry march, and his face couldn't hide his annoyance. He joined us at the table in silence, the silver fork and knife glistening in his hands as he stabbed the first piece of steak. I winced. It was then that I knew that I had made some mistake I wasn't aware of. I'd left the light on upstairs maybe. Or I'd been hoarding the scissors as usual; the pile of carefully cut paper dolls sat in a corner of my room on the second floor, next to my dirty clothes and books. My room! That's it! My unused knife slipped forgotten from my right hand. Only my sister noticed the nice clean clink it made as it hit the plate. Her eyes caught mine but I couldn't read any expression in her face. I hadn't cleaned my room while he was gone, and I think there was more than one apple core under the bed. The tangy smell didn't bother me, and it wasn't the season for ants, but of course he wouldn't accept it.

I wanted to eat my steak with salty gravy. Usually, I'd alternate bites of steak, corn, and peas, steak, corn, and peas, until all I had left were too many peas. Meanwhile, he was having no trouble eating his dinner, and with every angry jab of his fork, I felt less and less hungry. I counted the peas; there were forty-seven. How was anyone ever expected to eat forty-seven peas? They sat circling the steak on my plastic white plate with the blue elephant in the middle. The metal fork was warming in my left hand, and the steam had stopped rising from the plate.

Suddenly I knew what I had to do. I stood up abruptly, bumping the wooden table clumsily. "Be right back!" I shouted and skirted away. My father, mother, and sister all looked my way, confused, their heads with matching brown hair turned in unison. I didn't give them time to say anything. I just ran up the brown carpeted stairs to my small square bedroom on the second floor. I grabbed a trash can from the bathroom on the way, and hastily started throwing trash in it. I crawled under my bed and fished out the apple cores, my hands getting a little sticky. I gathered my paper dolls gingerly and discarded the scraps. Then I hoisted all my clothes into the closet in a big bunch, and struggled to close the door. When the door clicked shut, I surveyed my room. Not too bad, I thought. I'd have to make my bed later.

I marched back down to the dinner table, triumphant. My mother was carrying plates to the sink and my sister had moved over to the couch to watch TV. My father ruffled my hair as I passed, looking amused. "You've got paper scraps in your hair," he said. He exchanged a look with my mom, both their lips curling up slightly at the edges. I blushed as I sat down and finished my cold dinner with forty-seven peas.

ꕥ

Prompt: Red lentils, necklace with a dolphin and mood stone and a small bag of cotton balls.

By Bob Beckwith

This week's writing prompts are stacked against me. All three seem slanted towards female writers. Why should I be surprised? After all, our class consists of five women, one man, plus a female teacher.

Ok, ok, enough bellyaching, I must play the hand I've been dealt—so here goes. I have never cooked anything with red lentils. Now ladies, quit your giggling. Yes, I do cook—and very well I might add. Watch it—I can read your minds: You're thinking, yeah he cooks all right—like he knows how to rip open a box and shove the contents into the microwave. Wrong! I've actually been cooking since I was a youngster. Over the years, I've mastered many main dishes, soups and desserts—and all from scratch.

I will admit to having some learning experiences along the way, such as the time when I was eight years old. I decided to make a pound cake. My mother's handwritten recipe called for one egg—mixed on high. The only "high" I knew was on the electric stove. When I served the cake, my parents tactfully asked me what the little rubbery pieces were. Between gales of laughter, my mother explained that the "high" referred to her electric mixer—not the stove. Well, the birds liked the cake.

It blows my mind that a girl or a woman would even consider wearing a necklace containing a dolphin and a mood stone. I understand the dolphin part. They are beautiful creatures that have been used in jewelry for centuries by many cultures. Among other things, dolphins portray peacefulness, gentleness and harmony.

But what's with the mood stone? Why would anyone want to broadcast their emotional feelings? Yes, I do know how mood stones work. They change color based on an individual's body heat. Using this premise, let's assume a woman wears this necklace to a party where she hopes to portray herself as cool, calm and collected. Unfortunately there's a ton of people—"sardined" in a tiny room with no ventilation. In five blinks of an eye, her stone turns pitch black, screaming, "I'm uptight and hot!"

Or picture this scenario. A college gal wears her necklace to a cocktail party. This time the room is very comfortable, however, after a few drinks, a complete jerk of a guy starts putting the make on her. She becomes marginally heated trying tactfully to quell his advances, until he blurts out, "You know you want me—your mood stone is deep blue—the sign of passion."

And then there's that small bag of white, fluffy cotton balls—how disgusting. No not for how they might be used, but rather because they remind me of snow. God, haven't we had enough of that already? And speaking of snow, I like the sign found in front of a church last week. It read, "Whoever is praying for snow—would you please stop?!"

Well, so much for the female prompts. However, things could be worse. Mindy might have thrown in a male prompt, such as Cialis. I thought I knew why men might purchase this product—that is until I saw their ad on TV. The ad begins by showing a man and a woman getting a little dreamy-eyed and cozy while doing the laundry. The announcer states that, "An everyday moment can turn romantic at any time." This is followed by some tactful words explaining the benefits of Cialis. However, the very next scene shows the same couple—sans clothes, sitting in separate bathtubs, staring into each other's eyes, while holding hands on a deserted beach. If that's all Cialis did for them—then count me out. Oh—one last thing—where'd they get the water to fill the tubs?

ꟷ

Walgreens Poetry Slam

By Lisa R. Benson

The entire first paragraph was a prompt.

I turned my blue nineties station wagon into the driveway of the historic building for my writing class but instantly noticed something must be wrong. All the lights were out, the building abandoned like a school at Christmastime. In the dark, I reached across to the passenger seat and dug one hand into my purse until I could feel my calendar. I pulled out the tiny leather keeper-of-my-life, its once hard binder now worn from a year's worth of abuse. It was clearly time for the 2009 clone. I flipped on the dome light and hastily turned to December, flipping the pages best I could despite my thick leather gloves. Hmmm, right there in black ink it said class was scheduled, so I shut the car and worked my way to the door in the dark while wondering if my desire to write was worth all this hassle? I managed to find the door in the dark and pulled at the handle. Nothing; jammed shut. The only thing I could see was my breath creating steam. Ah a cup of hot tea would be nice, but noooo, I was out there in the cold, ice forming in my nostrils. Was it even safe standing there in darkness? How was Bedford's crime rate anyway? Just to be sure, I pushed my coat sleeve back and pressed the stem on my watch to light it up and double check the time: yup, six-thirty, the teacher and rest of the class surely should be here by now. I thought I'd just wait a bit more in the car, and started to walk when I suddenly recalled a second memo from the teacher saying, what was it?, oh shit, that's right, she had made an error and there was no class on December 11! It was meant to be December 18! And I bothered to dress and fix my makeup for nothing.

Well, I guess I could just go to Mindy's house.

First thing's first, I had to figure out where Mindy lived. What was her last name again? It's like that artist… Jackson something. Pollock! Pollock-Fusi. That's a pretty catchy name.

Back in my car, I decided to drive until I found a shop likely to have a phone book. I could look her up in the phone book and drive over there. I had spent an excruciating five hours that morning on the homework causing me to miss work and I really wanted to share it with someone.

Nearby I noticed a drugstore. They must have a phone book, right? I parked in the icy lot and entered the store. Inside were your usual cashiers, high school students who chatted or stared at the counter all night. I asked a girl behind the counter, "Do you have a phone book?"

"A phone book? Let me check. *Ned, do we have a phone book!?*" her voice screeched loudly in the direction of a tall man in the back who must have been the manager. It was all I could do not to cringe. I was starting to wonder if that hot cup of tea wasn't a better idea. Ned didn't hear her. He had bent over to pick up a rack of fallen magazines, the glossy covers sliding out of his hands and back into the floor. "For the love of God…" he was muttering.

"If you had a phone book, maybe it'd be behind the counter? Or by a pay phone, if you have one." The last time I had used a phone book that wasn't via internet had been years. All I could think of was the scene in Back to the Future where Marty goes into the café to look up Doc Brown when he accidentally ends up in the 1950s.

"Um, we don't have a pay phone…" said the girl uncertainly.

"Hmmm…" I muttered, tapping my finger on my chin. I didn't need Mindy to share my story. The world was full of people just waiting to be entertained, wasn't it? That's why they can charge ten dollars in the movie theaters now, and why the TV at home had more than two hundred channels. Two hundred channels and nothing to watch…

"Wanna hear a story?" I asked the girl. She looked up at me and for the first time I noticed her eyes: they were as blue as ice but not cold somehow.

"What do you mean?" she asked.

"Well, I'm a writer, and I wrote a story. It's not too long. Want to hear it?"

The girl looked behind me, as if expecting another customer to come to the counter. No one came. She shrugged, looking neither pleased nor displeased, just confused. "Sure," she said.

So, among cigarettes, candy bars, and gum displayed on the shelves in colorful containers, I read my story. Afterward her eyes were still looking down at the counter. She was fingering her necklace.

"Cool story," she said. "Can I help who's next?" she asked. A man behind me beckoned for cigarettes.

ഗ്രൈ

Hildegaard's Complaint

By Charlotte Christen

"It's too hot," Frieda complained. "You know the liquid should be tepid when the snakeskin is dropped into the cauldron. It says so right there on the tablet." Frieda continued, "You should have allowed that blood broth to cool a bit. Do you have everything else we need? Now, as soon as it cools, drop in the snakeskin, bring it to a boil again and then drop in the chameleon. I do hope you brought a well-fed one, they generally squirm and try to jump out when you drop them in, but if they're well fed and plump, they sink to the bottom."

Hildegaard listened to her older sister's monologue without rolling her eyes even a little. Frieda was far too serious about this crazy stuff; she was so bossy and rigid. Who cares that both of their parents were witches? Did they really need to learn all these potions to prove they were loyal to the family? She would never be able to remember all the chants in her textbook.

It was Hildegaard who was charged with the task of preparing the blood broth, that horribly smelly concoction. What a fiasco that turned out to be. Catching that damn chicken after chopping off its head was totally disgusting. She got dizzy chasing it around the yard and then after finally getting a firm grip on the feet it dripped blood all the way to the kettle; she managed at least to catch the required cup and a half. Then she needed to pluck out the feathers before she could cook it and she'd had no idea how to get the meat off of the bones. Frieda hadn't even cared that Hildegaard scorched her hair while bending over the bonfire to singe off the pinfeathers of that dumb bird. "Aaaagh!" The chameleon was swimming, not sinking. It must be immune to boiling broth. Splat. There now, a good whack with the wooden spoon was all it needed.

Hildegaard stopped stirring to look up at the stars. It was a beautiful night with an amazing full moon. Yes, she thought, there had to be a better line of work than witchery; this business of curses and hexes was as much her talent and passion as was painting a Picasso. Music, that's what she should study. She liked to sing along while she played her lute.

"For Hell's Sake, Hildegaard!" Frieda shrieked. "Would you please pay attention to stirring that pot? Now look at what you've done, the spiders broke loose from their seasoning bag and they're crawling all over my head, the blood broth has boiled away and the chameleon is burning to the bottom of the pot and, oh, Hildegaard, you are impossible. I told you it was too hot, I told you." Frieda stamped her pointy-toed high heeled witch boot so hard the ground beneath her shattered and she fell through to the next level of her existence.

"Well, I'll be damned," Hildegaard said, and a voice wheezed out from the ground, "You can count on it."

ᢒᢓ

The Tales of Tom Tom the Terrible

By Kathleen Shure

I saw her walking toward me, each step like an angry march, and her face couldn't hide her annoyance. I was crouched under the chair, my head practically down on the ground, waiting for her to whack me on the head. I had really done it this time. She said, "You are dead meat!" It wasn't my fault that she left the wire door open while getting fresh water! But, oh, I couldn't help myself, what was behind the door had made such a good lunch! And I almost *was* dead meat, since after she whacked me on the head (because a bunch of feathers were sticking out of my mouth), I almost choked on a canary bone! I tried to say "meow" but I couldn't, and she took pity on me and grabbed me around my middle and pushed up, so there I was, the recipient of the Heimlich maneuver on a cat!

Oh, but wait until tomorrow when she cleans the fish tank !

ꕥ

7

RELATIONSHIPS

Pinky and Alice

By Rhona Barlevy

Pinky watched as the sands of time poured through the shapely little hourglass. It sat on the kitchen windowsill, where it had been for almost thirty-five years, counting seconds and minutes, one glistening grain at a time. Pinky dreaded the last grain as he knew he wasn't ready. Judging from the mess on the kitchen table, and pretty much everywhere else, he was never going to get done on time.

Whatever had made him think he could do this, invite Alice for coffee and cake like it was an everyday normal thing? Since his wife, Naomi, had died a year ago, Pinky had had no one to the house. And now looking around the disheveled and not very clean kitchen, he began to realize how bizarre his life had gotten. The house had become quite cluttered and it required considerable caution to navigate the rooms. Naomi's possessions and personal items were everywhere like treasured artifacts. He just could not bring himself to dispose of or give any of it away. Naomi's death had been very sudden and quite shocking and her things were frozen in place where she had last left them. A pair of mushy soft scuffed loafers sat tucked under the couch. A red cabled cardigan, her favorite, remained hanging off the arm of the worn brown leather club chair. "The Joy Luck Club," a favorite novel, lay on the table next to the chair, still open to the last page she had been reading. And a bright yellow tea cup with dried rusty rings of tea visible within, sat beside the book. On top of all of this he had really been unable to put away anything new that entered the house. A package of light bulbs lay open on the dining room table, left there after he had fixed a lamp. In addition, toilet paper, paper towels and kitchen soap were keeping the light bulbs company. Judging from the continuous array of dirty dishes and implements lining the kitchen counters, Pinky had yet to even use the kitchen soap he had purchased. In fact, every horizontal surface of the kitchen was covered with something. He had, however, managed to carve out a small space on the dinette table to eat his meager meals. As he surveyed this overwhelming disarray, Pinky feared he was becoming like those hoarder folks he watched on reality television. People whose homes were so cluttered with possessions not even any floor showed through.

"Well," he thought with some relief as he looked down, "I can see my floor; it's filthy but I can see it."

Naomi had been his anchor in the world. The plump sweet creamy roundness of her face, the chocolate brown eyes rimmed in long dark lashes, the generous mouth always talking, laughing, and her tumble of messy wavy brown hair gave him a comfort and peace he knew nowhere else. Pinky was, and had always been, very socially awkward. He had hardly dated in his youth, and when his friend Bernie had wanted to set him up on a blind date with a woman from his office, he had really resisted. But Bernie was unrelenting; he insisted this woman was the one for Pinky. And so, finally, he had succumbed and gone on the date. Bernie, it turns out, had been right. The second Pinky walked into the restaurant and saw Naomi sitting at the table, he knew it too. He took one look at those cheeks and those eyes and felt that he was home. Naomi apparently had not shared that feeling, and many dates later revealed to Pinky that she had not wanted to go out with him again after that first blind date. That evening, despite his feelings about her, he had sat mutely tucked into the corner of the booth, torturing his napkin into various shapes and making almost no eye contact. He did laugh a few times at Bernie's jokes, but had essentially left Bernie and Myra to entertain Naomi. It was her mother, Esther, who had convinced Naomi to give him a second chance. Pinky had been forever grateful to Esther for that, and also her incredible cooking. She cooked all the traif foods that were not allowed in his kosher orthodox Jewish home. When he was invited to Naomi's parents for dinner, Esther often made him the most deliciously seasoned pork chops or her famous lobster Newburg. She had a way with turning even the most mundane hamburger into a savory treat. As it turned out, Naomi hadn't inherited her mother's culinary talents, however Pinky loved to cook and Esther was delighted to teach him many of her recipes and tricks. But now, he seldom cooked; he ate plain meals that he barely tasted. And he had lost weight since Naomi died. It was now necessary to cinch his belts tight around his waist to keep his pants up. He knew he looked pretty bedraggled these days but just didn't care, for he had lost his best friend, and what anyone else thought just didn't matter.

Pinky roused himself from his reverie, looked up once more at the little hour glass on the window sill. And as he watched more sand fall through to the bottom, again he drifted off. This time he went back to an early morning two years ago when he had come into the kitchen and found Naomi kneeling on the floor in tears. The hourglass was lying next to her with its red top cracked and sand pouring out onto the floor. She was apparently trying to scoop up the sand with a teaspoon.

"What's wrong?" he had asked, alarmed at her tears.

"This was my mother's favorite for timing eggs. It fell and broke and I can't fix it!" she cried. Naomi's grief was almost palpable. He had helped her up and sat her on a kitchen chair, and then set about gluing the cracked top and putting the sand back inside.

"Oh Pinky you can fix anything," she had said, her tears now dry and her eyes and mouth crinkled in a wide smile. Naomi had then set the timer back on the window sill where it still remained, continuing to mark the passage of time. He surmised, focusing on the crack in the top, that the repair had worked out just fine, as the hour glass had lasted longer than both Naomi and her mother.

As Pinky dried his own tears from his eyes, he heard a light gentle tapping coming from the back door. He rose, cleared a few dishes from the table and placed them in the pile by the sink. Then he headed toward the door where he could see Alice's face in the storm door window. She looked lovely, backlit by the porch light. It made a sort of a halo around her short blonde curls and gave her plump pink cheeks a warm glow. He took a deep breath, exhaled slowly, then opened the door. What else could he do?

Alice entered the kitchen and handed him a delicious spicy-smelling bakery box. She then turned and surveyed the room. He could see her eyes wide with surprise and perhaps even a little shock.

"I'm sorry, I'm sorry it's such a mess," Pinky said, looking more at the floor than at Alice. "It all just seems to have gotten away from me." He continued, still looking down at the floor.

"Well," said Alice, "It is a bit of a mess, but I think we can get these dishes washed up, put some of these things away and make some space for ourselves."

Pinky was astounded. He had expected her to bolt out the door at the sight of the kitchen, and she hadn't even seen the rest of the place. But what surprised him even more was that he accepted her offer. He found an empty space on top of the refrigerator in which to place the bakery box, and then went into the dining room to retrieve the dish soap and paper towels from their table top residence. "You know Alice, I really thought you would turn and run when you saw this mess." He said as he walked back into the kitchen.

"You've had a hard year. And it's not as bad as you think. It's mostly a lot of clutter, and the rest just needs soap, water and a little elbow grease. You and Naomi always had a lovely home and soon it will be again." Alice spoke in a kind comforting voice; she could see he was tearing up.

"I really loved Naomi," Pinky choked out.

"I know," said Alice softly, "or I wouldn't be here."

He sat down heavily in one of the kitchen chairs, his shoulders slumped forward and his hands clenched together.

"It's not your fault," Alice continued. "We can't know all or be everywhere. All we can do is love people and care for them."

"Perhaps," he said sadly. "But she was all alone when it happened, and the guilt is so heavy and hard inside me. I feel like it has carried me to the bottom of the ocean, and it weighs so much I can't swim back up." His tears were now flowing down his face.

Alice sat in the chair next to him and gently rubbed his arm. "How could you possibly know what would happen to Naomi that day? She was perfectly fine and healthy. There were no symptoms of the aneurysm. The doctors said things like that can go undetected for years."

"I don't know, I keep going over it in my head. There must have been some sign. If only I had been here," Pinky said as he wiped at his tears.

"Even if you had been, the doctors said it was over in an instant, what could you have done?" Alice responded.

Pinky sighed and placed his hand over hers as it rested on his forearm. "You know what, that cake smells very delicious, let's get started cleaning up so we can have space to pig out on it."

Alice gave a little laugh. "That sounds good to me, let's do it." So he got up, put on the radio, and they set to work companionably. About halfway through, Alice picked up the little hourglass and flipped it over, smiling as the sand ran through it. She turned to Pinky with a sad sort of wistful look on her face and said, "You know my mother had one just like this one and I played with it all the time when I was a child."

"Really?" said Pinky. "That one was Naomi's Mom's. It's funny, the little memories that stay with us and keep us company."

Alice smiled as she returned the hourglass to the windowsill. Soon, a lot quicker than he had expected, the counters were clear, the sink empty and the table shining. Pinky then started the coffee, using the newly unearthed electric pot, while Alice set the table and retrieved the cake box from the top of the refrigerator. Shortly, the room was suffused with delicious odors he had not smelled in a long time. He also realized that he felt something he had not felt in an even longer time, a sense of contentment. He looked up at Alice's sweet face smiling back at him from across the table and thought that maybe, just maybe, he could find a way to swim back up.

The rest of the evening went quickly. They sipped their coffee and talked about Alice's husband Arthur, who had passed away almost three years before. She was surprisingly open about what a difficult and cranky person he could be at times.

"I'm surprised," Pinky told her. "I never saw that side of him, he was always so funny."

"He was," she admitted. "Arthur's humor, especially his 'knock knock' jokes got us through some of his more difficult moods. My favorite was the one he always used when he knew I was at my wits end with him."

"What one was that?" he asked.

"It was one Arthur would say just as I was about to yell at him. 'Knock, knock,'" she said, looking up at Pinky.

"Who's there?" he said, playing along.

"Don't cha," she replied.

"Don't cha who?" he answered back.

"Don't cha know I love you?" Alice finished the joke with tears shining in her eyes.

"I can see," he said in a soft voice, "why that was your favorite."

"Yeah," she whispered as she reached across the table to cut another piece of cake. Then Alice lightened the mood and told him a story about the time she and Naomi were grocery shopping, and she found Naomi's car keys stuck in with the grapefruits in the produce section of the market.

"Naomi was famous for leaving her car keys places, but I never heard that one." Pinky laughed and then told Alice, "Once, when I came home from work, I opened the freezer to get some ice cubes, and there were Naomi's car keys sitting next to the ice cream."

"You know," said Alice as she shook her head and laughed, "I think you could write some funny stories about Naomi and her car keys."

They chatted a bit longer, and as the evening was coming to an end, he found himself reluctant to let her go. Then Alice surprised him, as she was gathering her belongings, she leaned over, gave him a little whisper of a kiss on the cheek, and said, "How about next Sunday we tackle the dining room?"

Pinky felt his heart soar and he said, "And you know what? Afterwards I'll make us dinner. I don't know if you remember, but I'm quite a good cook."

"Yes, I do remember," she said, laughing. Then just as she was turning to leave, Pinky walked to the windowsill and retrieved the little hourglass.

"Here," he said, handing it to her. "Be a child again."

Alice's face lit up. "Are you sure?" she said.

"Absolutely," he replied, then kissed her on the cheek and said goodnight.

After Alice left, he cleared the dishes, washed them, and put them in the dish drain. As he was drying his hands on the dishtowel, he surveyed the resurrected kitchen. He shook his head in disbelief. When the day began, he would never have predicted this outcome. But there were many things he never thought would happen and yet they did.

"Well, there is something I can predict for sure," thought Pinky. "Tomorrow I will go to Macy's and buy some pants that fit and a smart new shirt." Then he closed the kitchen light and headed up to bed.

ꕥ

The Bestseller

By Karen Bella

"You'll never meet anyone who will be as nice and kind to you as I was. Oh well, as far as I'm concerned, it's your loss!"

Anne thought of the email Jackie had sent her three years before. The words in the email hurt, but Jackie was wrong! Anne's life was full of good people and happiness.

Anne wondered if the situation with her college roommate could have turned out better if she had communicated with Jackie. Their friendship really had taken a turn years prior when the two girls had met for lunch at Bertucci's.

On that particular Saturday, Anne was upset. The day before, she had been laid off from the job she had worked at for thirteen years. She thought Jackie would be a good friend who would listen and be compassionate. The waiter came and took their order. They always ordered pepperoni pizza. Jackie ordered lemonade and Anne ordered a Pepsi. It was just like a regular Saturday get-together. Anne told Jackie what happened to her, and Jackie listened, but that was all she did. She never offered Anne any words of encouragement.

Anne was fully aware of the other people in the restaurant, and wondered what they were talking about. Were they having give-and-take communication? Anne needed to have a conversation at that moment. The drinks came and then the salad and the pizza, but the entire time, Anne was feeling very uncomfortable. She had thought it would be a good idea to get out instead of staying home feeling miserable. But now she was having second thoughts about meeting Jackie. How, she wondered, could Jackie be acting as though she didn't care that Anne was going through a bad time? Anne knew that if the situation were different, if Jackie had lost her job, Anne would ask how she was doing, and what she was going to do next. Anne knew she would be interested in the well-being of a friend. Jackie continued to show no emotion, causing Anne to feel frustrated.

Jackie was drinking her third lemonade and had already eaten three slices of pizza. Anne wasn't hungry, so she had barely finished her first slice of pizza. Maybe, she thought, it would be better to talk about other things. She asked Jackie what was new with her.

Suddenly, Jackie came to life.

"I'm getting my own classroom!" she exclaimed. Jackie had been working in daycare and was just given a great opportunity. As Jackie continued to speak, she became very animated. Even though Anne had asked how Jackie was doing, she resented how her so-called friend only wanted to talk about herself. It wouldn't have mattered what Jackie said about Anne being laid off; it would have been better than saying nothing at all.

Unfortunately, there were more get-togethers like this one at Bertucci's. Anne would have liked to confide in Jackie, but she no longer felt comfortable in the friendship.

One year later, after a lot of frustration, Anne decided to send Jackie an email letting her know the friendship was over. Anne had to move forward, but she wished Jackie the best in her future. Anne had no ill feelings toward Jackie, so Jackie's response was a shock. Anne didn't understand how Jackie could be so vicious.

Here Anne sat at the bookstore, preparing to do a signing for her debut bestseller, and she realized she had made the best decision to end her friendship with Jackie. Over the years, Anne hardly thought about where Jackie was because Anne was too busy with her marriage and children. Her family was all that mattered to her. She wouldn't have thought about Jackie that night either if she hadn't looked up to see Jackie standing in line waiting to have a copy of her book signed....

Madame Tussauds Wax Museum

By Marilou Barsam

Sitting on my back deck, sipping merlot as the sun slowly sets behind our tree-studded hill, I think I hear Lily once again mentioning President Obama's name.

It amuses me that she is so taken with him; after all, being only seven, she definitely has no strong political affiliations. And in general, she is not one to be swept off her feet with celebrity-dom. Unlike her peers, she has never mentioned Hanna Montana.

Yet since his campaign, it was obvious to me Lily was drawn to him, as if she understood what was so special about him, as if she sensed his uniqueness; not necessarily within the context of his presidential predecessors but more related to his not being typical like everyone else.

I've stopped counting the Obama portraits she has drawn in school and at home. There is tall stick-figure Obama, with his Abe Lincoln-like stature; and there is short and squat Obama, of the Odo Star-Trek type, sometimes sporting a bright red tie, but always dressed in black with a black complexion complete with nubby-like black hair and that consistent smile of effervescent white teeth.

Her mini-cartoons often feature a guest appearance from none other than the President himself. He may be interrupting a conversation between a cat and a dog, or making a dramatic entry to help banish a sinister character Lily has conjured up.

Being the analytical person I am, I find it hard to take her fascination with the President at face value. Could it be Barack (which she occasionally uses to refer to him) has served to fill something special in her life?

Recently we travelled to London, England and all agreed we should include Madame Tussauds wax museum in our itinerary.

As we toured each floor, marveling at the true-to-life figures of movie stars, sports icons, and political giants, Lily enjoyed recognizing and meeting many of the carefully-molded personalities she identified with from TV and the movies. At Michael Jackson's figure she "struck a pose" imitating his. At Queen Elizabeth's she politely curtsied, playing and pretending that each figure somehow recognized her as well.

But it was when we all realized that President Obama was actually in a simulated oval office—standing tall as a tower, arms crossed, big smile—did she shed her theatrical pose.

Before we could blink, she flew across the waxed and slippery floor, with her bright orange crocks flopping furiously under her feet, until she came to a grinding halt in front of him.

And then breaking the museum's rules—which she previously had reminded us of many times—she lovingly flung her arms around his hips and gently placed her head against his crisply tailored pants. And there she stood, squeezing him and smiling at him as if waiting for him to return the gesture.

The museum photographer was so taken by the scene, she told her to "freeze" and took her picture, luckily for us capturing this moment forever after. This photograph proudly sits in our breakfast nook now so that Lily can admire it as she gulps down her morning orange juice.

Somehow I feel like the Frommer's Guide got it all wrong when they discouraged visits to Madame Tussauds, citing the museum as "offering no cultural value whatsoever." Evidently they overlooked the pricelessness of the museum's ability to offer a young girl the opportunity to connect with a hero figure in an intimate way.

༄

Love Again

By Jennifer Klein

The water hissed from the faucet as Bruce turned it on to a medium trickle. He reached for the white oval bar of soap and applied it to his palms. Replacing the bar, he lathered suds on both sides of his hands and in between his fingers. With his round brush he gave his fingernails a quick scrub. As the water made its last satisfying gurgle down the sink, he pulled the towel from the towel ring and patted his hands thoroughly before neatly replacing the towel.

Looking in the mirror, he quickly combed his long white mustache then he brushed his curly white hair and gave it a final pat. "Not bad," he told his reflection as he stepped back and flashed himself a smile.

At fifty-eight, he was still quite handsome. Some of his old friends had lost their looks, but that, he knew, was mostly due to weight. "Your body is your temple," his father had always told him and his brother Rich. He had said it so often that the two boys started using it in their repertoire, cracking themselves up over their parents' idiosyncrasies. But every day since his fortieth birthday Bruce had thanked his old man for that bit of advice.

Bruce slipped his black leather jacket over his navy wool sweater and checked the collar of his Oxford shirt in the hall mirror. Still straight. He zipped up his jacket, and leaving his tidy two-story Victorian, he made his way up the twelve blocks to the party.

The moon was a bright yellow lantern in the sky. Scattered wooly gray clouds seemed to march toward it, pushed by the strength of the dense winds, which were warm for October. He could see the porch lights on at Kathy and Dennis's house.

"Bruce! You made it!" Dennis called, waving to him from the front porch. Bruce bounded the last few steps toward his friend's warm handshake. "How are you?" Dennis asked.

Bruce touched Dennis's shoulder with his left hand as he shook hands with his right. "Never better. How about you? You and Kathy keeping yourselves well?"

"Doing our best!" Dennis said, crossing his feet as he leaned against the porch railing.

"Wonderful. You've got to tell me when you start running again, Dennis. I miss our afternoon chats."

"Of course. I've got a few months of swimming and weights and then it's back to spring and summer running and cycling. You know the drill. I've got to mix it up a little."

"Good man," Bruce said.

Go on in and make yourself at home. Kathy's been waiting for you." He gave Bruce a warm smile. "I'll be in in a few minutes. I'm on greeting duty."

Bruce nodded heartily. He took an invigorating deep breath, smelling the sweet autumn smell of decaying leaves.

Inside, he was greeted with a friendly wave of contemporary jazz and the cozy smell of a warm fire. The lights were turned down low and white votive candles flickered in their glass candle holders throughout the room.

A group of twelve were huddled around the tufted brown leather coffee table sitting on blue and green upholstered chairs, a cream colored couch, and stools squeezed in to provide extra seating. Rita and Lorraine were speaking in the hushed tones of expert storytellers. Lorraine's husband, Jim, was chuckling quietly in anticipation of the punchline. Rita and Lorraine called it out together, "They bathed us everywhere!!"

The crowd let out a loud laugh.

"*Absolutely* everywhere!" Lorraine repeated. "It was a bit of an orgasmic massage. Pardon my bluntness, there. I suppose that's where the 'glow' in 'salt glow' comes from. But a word to the wise! Don't sign up for spa services without asking what they entail."

Jim sheepishly added, "Based on Lorraine's mood when she got home..." Jim cleared his throat, "I want to recommend that every man buy their wife a gift certificate for a salt glow." He chuckled heartily.

Bruce laughed from behind the group, "This is quite a conversation I'm walking into!"

Rita looked up from the group. "Bruce!" she called.

"Rita." Bruce smiled and exhaled through his nose, walking in long strides toward the couch. "How are you doing?"

~~~

"Rita... How are you doing?" He had said those same words six months earlier as Rita sat on this same couch. It was a spring afternoon. The robins and sparrows called merrily around the bird feeder in the yard, and the last rays of the afternoon sun stretched across the floor spotlighting a few flakes of dust that had escaped Kathy's attention. The room appeared dark and gray against the golden glow on the floor. Rita was sitting in a tired heap against Kathy's willing shoulder. Kathy had her arms wrapped in support around her friend. Rita blew her nose and crumpled the tissues into her fist. Wiping away the tears with her manicured index finger, she looked up at Bruce.

"There, there," Kathy had said, patting Rita's auburn head.

Rita's breath hitched as she inhaled deeply and looked back down, trying not to start weeping again.

Bruce walked across the room, sat on the arm of the couch, and rested his warm hand on Rita's back. "I know," he had said.

~~~

In the evening glow of the party, Kathy was quickly by his side. "Bruce. I'm so glad you're here! Come get a drink." Bruce surveyed the glasses of the guests around the room. Mostly reds, some white. Rita and Lorraine would be drinking Prosecco, he knew.

"Save my spot!" he told Rita.

Rita tilted her head toward him and smiled. "Sure thing."

~~~
~~~

Bruce had been sitting in his house that spring day, enjoying, and sometimes not enjoying, or maybe angrily enjoying, one of the better political books to come out in the past year.

"Unbelievable," he had said, for probably the tenth time that afternoon, when the phone rang.

"Probably a fundraiser," he announced to no one, still riled up from his reading. He walked across the room to the phone to check. The caller ID read, "Leahy."

Bruce picked up the phone. "Hello!" he said, expecting to hear Dennis's voice. They'd had a great run that morning—six miles—with as many hills as they could find on their way, "Great for the hamstrings!" Dennis always said. Bruce was looking forward to the next day's run.

But it was Kathy's voice on the other end. "Hi Bruce," she said quietly. "I don't know if I should tell you this or not.... But... I think you should know."

"What is it?" he asked, his heart pounding vigorously.

"It's Rita," Kathy said. Then words seemed to spill out faster than Bruce could interpret them. "Gary and Rita have split up. Gary's left her for some tart at the tennis club. A twenty-five year old. He's got her knocked up. He has the gall to call her 'the love of his life.' A twenty-five year old? Can you believe that bastard?"

"Where is she? Where is Rita right now?" Bruce asked.

"She's coming over. I don't think you should come. I am so furious with that s.o.b. I don't know if Rita would want me to tell you, but I thought you should know. Poor Rita. Oh... Here she is now...gotta go."

"I'll be right there," he blurted as the receiver clicked on Kathy's end.

He felt a dull ache in his stomach and head, and a desperate thirst overwhelmed him. Bruce plodded to the kitchen, the tapping of his hard-soled slippers against the hardwood floor thumping in his ears with his every step. He pulled a glass from the cabinet and pushed the cabinet door shut. The resulting slam made him jump. He filled the glass with water from the pitcher on the counter and guzzled it. Still thirsty. He filled his glass again and placed the empty pitcher on the counter. He guzzled a second glass of water. Still thirsty. He filled his glass from the tap and drank that. His stomach felt full with sloshing water, but still he was thirsty. He wondered if there were something from his medicine cabinet that could get rid of this feeling.

Instead, he grabbed his keys, quickly changed into his shoes and walked out the front door. The rich smell of new spring growth flooded his nose as he locked his front door. He turned and stared at the steps of his front porch.

He remembered how he and Rita had sat on that front porch together on the day she had moved out fifteen years before.

~~~

"We could have had it all," Bruce had told her as they sat together on those gray porch steps— their porch for the last time. He had placed his face in his hands and then ran his fingers through his hair, brown mixed with an occasional gray.

"Everything except children," Rita told him resolutely from behind her sunglasses. "You can still make this right."

"You know I can't," he said with his voice choked with tears. "I love children, but I love other people's children. I really don't want to bring any of my own into this world. It's a crazy place, and it's getting crazier by the day."

"But your children..." she started, but then corrected herself, "Our children.... Our children could help make this world a better place!"

"Rita, no. I don't. I can't. I'm sorry." He looked at cracks in the paint. He couldn't bear to see her sadness. He didn't want her to see his. She knew how he felt about children—how he had always felt. It really was unfair of her to ask him to change his mind just because she had changed hers. This wasn't changing the paint color in the bathroom, for God's sake. But now that she had changed her mind, she was leaving. This was her last chance, she had said. She was thirty-five and it was now or never. It was her prerogative.

She sighed sadly, standing up, and pushed her hair behind her ears. "We had a good run didn't we?"

"The best." He tried to smile. His heart already ached with missing her.

She pushed her lips together in her own forced smile, and she turned and walked away.

Bruce hung his arms over his knees and watched her walk to her silver Honda Accord, packed with the last of her things. The warm
~~~

summer breeze carried the sweet smell of all those flowers they had planted together in May.

'Lovely Rita', he thought as she opened her car door. "I miss you already!" he called out before he knew he was doing it. It was such an understatement, of course he missed her already. He missed their future. He missed sharing their past.

She held up her hand in a kind-of a wave before she drove away from his house for the last time.

"You'll be back!" he called to the back of her car, although he knew she couldn't hear him, and he didn't believe it himself.

~~~

Bruce looked down at his porch steps one last time, remembering all those years ago, and began his walk to Kathy's house, and to Rita.

At the party, Bruce followed Kathy away from the group in the living room and into the kitchen where several bottles of red wine were lined up next to the wine glasses on the white marble counter.

"Red?" Kathy asked, gesturing toward the wine bottles. "Or we have white in the refrigerator still, and Prosecco, of course."

"I'll have the Malbec," Bruce said, reaching for a glass.

Kathy poured. "Some night, huh?"

"So warm tonight! I'm starting to wonder if it will ever get cold this year."

"I know, I know." She frowned and wrapped her arms across her chest. "Are you working on any climate proposals?"

"I'm thinking of a new project, actually. I've got an idea for a white paper...."

A cheerful voice bellowed into the kitchen. "Bruce!" Hugh had just arrived. He held out his hand and shook Bruce's with one quick strong shake. "Kathy," he said, as he leaned over to kiss her hello.

"Is Ken here too, or are you flying solo tonight?" Bruce asked.

"Ken's called off for tonight. He's not feeling so well. What's this I hear about a new white paper?" The Pinot Noir gulped as Hugh poured it into his glass.

"Bruce is going to save the planet," Kathy told him.

"Well somebody's got to," Hugh said, shaking his head. "Have you felt how warm it is out there tonight? I just hope it's not too late. I've been thinking. Remember all those stories we were told as
~~~

boys, 'When I was your age I had to walk two miles to school through five feet of snow...'"

"Right! Without shoes," Bruce interrupted, finishing the tale. He took a sip of his Malbec.

"Right. Well I've been wondering if there was some truth to that, if the warming hadn't started much earlier, but it just moved at a slower pace, so people told these stories, but their children thought they were exaggerating."

Kathy added, "I remember reading the Little House on the Prairie books as a girl and wondering why *we* were never snowbound. At least once in those books, it had snowed so much that the Ingalls couldn't even open the door. They were stuck in the house, and Laura's father had to dig both their house and the barn out of the snow."

"It's all just happening faster now so we're more aware of it," Hugh said.

"You know," Kathy leaned back against the counter, "Since it is occurring faster now, maybe at least people will really be convinced that it's happening, and they'll be compelled to do something."

Bruce smoothed his mustache. "But still," he said, "some people still don't notice it or don't care. They get used to it so quickly. They say, 'nice day we're having today.' And I wish I could say—if it weren't so damned depressing and argumentative—I wish I could say, 'Well it feels good, but an eight-five-degree-day in October, or sixty degree-day in January, has a steep price. You may not be aware of it now, but soon enough we all will. Starting with Africa, Australia, and our own California. Hell! Africa and Australia are already aware of it. They're having the worst droughts they've ever seen.'" He took another sip of his Malbec.

Hugh added, "It wouldn't be such an uphill battle if it were global cooling instead of global warming."

"I've had that thought myself," Bruce added.

"Maybe Kathy's right. Maybe now that it's happening faster, more people will be concerned."

"Unfortunately, it seems it will have to happen a lot faster for people to really become concerned. The political will is so against change or even caring."

"It's the capitalist system. If it costs a buck, it can't be done." Hugh shook his head and put down his glass firmly.

"Well that's another topic altogether. I think we covered the fleecing of America at your last party, Kathy." Bruce smiled.

"Always a meeting of the minds! I'm so happy to have such brilliant friends," Kathy said. "Now if only I could get one or two of them to run for office, this country would be a much better place."

"You could always run, yourself," Bruce said.

Kathy's eyes sparkled as she grimaced. "Bruce, you know they would eat me alive! I can't think on my feet at all. You two on the other hand..." She looked back and forth between Bruce and Hugh, smiling. "But sadly, we can't solve all of the world's problems from my kitchen—at least not tonight, so let's see who else has arrived." She smoothed her long skirt, and gestured the men toward the living room.

"If only we could," Hugh muttered as they followed Kathy's lead.

~~~

It was just this past June when Bruce had helped Rita move out of the home she had shared with Gary and into her own apartment.

"You know," Bruce had asked, setting down his box next to her couch, "You could have just moved..."

Rita stopped in her tracks. She was still holding the last box from her car. "Don't even say it," she said, interrupting him. A smile lit up her face. It was the first smile he'd seen her wear in weeks.

"...into my place. I have plenty of space. You know, I even have an extra room." He finished, folded his arms across his chest.

Rita shook her head at him as Bruce helped her gently stack her last box on top of three others. "You're too good for that, Bruce. You can't be my rebound man. Besides, it's been fifteen years. We can't just pick up where we left off."

"I know. Although I wish we could," Bruce stood close to her and gently pushed a tendril of her hair across her forehead and back into place. "I just want you to know, whatever you need, I'll be there for you. The sky's the limit."

"I appreciate that," she said with her arms crossed. She sat down on her couch, already unpacked and tidy, and she looked up at him. "You know through all of the mess I went through with Gary— I have to tell you, thinking of you was such a comfort to me. When I first suspected Gary was up to something, of course I regretted not having stayed with you all those years ago. But that feeling of regret
~~~

disappeared quickly, because, you know, I had a life with Gary. I had a good life— a great life at times. I still can't believe he threw it all away." She paused, and Bruce could see her fighting to regain her composure. After a few seconds, she continued, "But you know, as soon as I remembered that my life with Gary was good, up until that point of course, the regret I had for leaving you disappeared. But do you know what it was replaced with?"

Bruce sat on the couch next to her and leaned forward, looking intently into her face. "What?"

"Comfort. The comfort of knowing that even though my marriage was collapsing, you would still be there for me. Might be there for me again. That we might even get a second chance."

"And you're sure you don't just want to move into my place..." he teased her.

"Bruce!" She rolled her eyes at him.

"I know." He smiled. It was actually too soon for him too.

~~~

Stretching in his bed with his arms under his pillow this past September Saturday, Bruce had felt the coolness of the sheets under him. He rolled over and propped his chin up on his hand, watching Rita sleep with the sheet tucked under her chin. Her hair, still curly, was redder now than it had been all of those years ago. He liked this new color. Her face was older, just as he knew his own was. Every year, time had removed a little more of the shine of youth, and yet now time seemed to be going backwards, because here she was again, with him.

The night before, everything had seemed so right between them, but with the morning always so awkward and uncertain, he wasn't ready to hope that she was coming back for good. Losing Rita had been so hard the first time, harder than he ever would have imagined. He couldn't let his heart hope for permanence yet.

He remembered how they had kissed last night. They had stood at the bottom of her front steps, the porch light dim above them. They were still talking, still not saying goodbye, and she had leaned her body in closer and closer to his. He felt her breath on his mustache hairs.

"I think I'm ready," she said, pulling her arms around him, pushing her body against his.
~~~

He cradled her in his arms, and leaned his forehead against hers. "Are you sure?" he asked. "I don't want to take advantage...."

They had spent the chilly early September evening together eating at an outside table at Mario's. They drank too much wine as the evening turned into night and they sat by the glow of the flickering candle lights. Rita, finally wanting to discuss Gary, told Bruce about the miscarriages, their decision after four losses just to travel and enjoy life as a sophisticated childless couple. She told him about their vacations together, where something always seemed to be missing. She told him about Gary's suddenly working longer hours at the office, and taking more business trips. And finally, she told him how Gary told Rita that he was going to be a father after all. Ashleigh's child. When she told Bruce, she hadn't cried. She told him with a resignation that he hadn't expected.

"Maybe it was just meant to be," she had said, leaning forward and looking at Bruce. He knew she had to think that way to avoid feeling further heartache, but he also knew he wanted her back, and he was glad to have the chance.

And then there she was with her body pressed up against his at her doorstep, saying "I *am* ready. And I need you."

He leaned forward, tickling her lips with his white mustache hairs, like he used to do all those years ago when they were brown, and he waited, imagining her anticipation and feeling his own before their lips parted and they kissed.

~~~

"That was the best trip of my life," Rita said, unfastening her seatbelt. She turned to face Bruce. He had turned the car off. "You know, I would move to Barcelona in a heartbeat. If you would move there with me."

"It was pretty great," he agreed.

"Pretty great?" she asked, making no move to get out of the car. "That city was better than any I've ever even imagined. Three restaurants dedicated to chocolate?"

"Which we hit three times each."

"Well, we just had to." She laughed. "It was a mission!"

Bruce laughed, slouching comfortably in his own seat.

"So, Mr. Dark and Mysterious..." Rita began, looking down.
~~~

Bruce hadn't expected the change in conversation. "Yes?" he asked.

"You never did tell me what happened to your Spanish beauty." Rita lifted her eyebrows up.

"Oh, Lucia..."

"Lucia," she repeated, "Yes. I've told you all about Gary. I need to hear what happened with Lucia. Why aren't you two still together?"

Lucia hadn't been far from his mind that day, actually. "It was on a day like today," he said, looking at Rita and then out the front window of the car. "We had just come back from Hawaii. We had had a great time—snorkeling, sailing, exploring volcanoes, relaxing on the beach, enjoying the romance of Hawaii. But when I got to her place, we were both ready to get back to our own lives. She even joked that she was glad I hadn't moved in because she had to get back into work mode. And I found myself wondering if I could ever see myself living with Lucia, and the truth was that I was looking forward to getting away from her, and I think she must have felt the same way. So things kind of died down after Hawaii. Still, I always wanted to see Barcelona. She always told me how wonderful it was."

"Well, I have to agree with her there," Rita said, slumping farther down into her seat, stretching a bit. "Oh, I really don't want to leave. I don't want to go back to the real world. I don't want to go back to work."

"I don't want you to leave either. I was thinking about the difference between my feelings between this vacation and the trip to Hawaii with Lucia. I want to be with you all of the time, Rita. We should think about getting a place together again."

Tears came to her eyes, and she smiled. "Oh Bruce," she said, but then her voice trailed off. She looked at the floor and then at Bruce again. "I was going to say that I'm too old to move in with anyone..." She paused. "You know that I want to be with you, but I'm just not sure about moving in yet." She sat up. "Let me think about it. Are you going to Kathy and Dennis's party after work tomorrow night?"

He felt his heart sink. He had been around long enough to know what was right, and this was right. But he didn't want to push her. He couldn't. He nodded in response.

"I'll meet you there. We can talk about it after."

~~~

At the party, Bruce carried his Malbec back to the couch and leaned on the arm next to Rita.

"I have an announcement to make, everyone," Rita said as she indicated to Lorraine and Jim to squeeze together on the couch to make room for Bruce. Bruce nestled in next to her as the noise of the party died down.

Rita stood up, smoothing her black dress as she turned to face Bruce. "Bruce," she said, tucking her hair behind her ear the way she always did. "You've been with me through thick and thin. As they say in the songs, 'You are my everything,' and I'd like you to marry me."

Bruce laughed out loud, and his eyes teared. For once he was speechless, and for just a second the crowd around them seemed to have melted away. But when he glanced around the room, all of their friends were smiling at him expectantly.

"What do you say, Bruce. Will you be my husband?" She bent down on one knee and rested her hands on his lap.

Shaking his head in disbelief, Bruce held both of her hands in his. "Rita," he said, "Sixteen years ago I let the best part of my life slip away, and every day I've suffered for it. Of course I will marry you."

"It's about time!" Kathy called from the back of the room, and Hugh gave a two-fingered whistle.

"How about next week?" Lorraine called above the crowd. "Jim became an ordained minister through the internet, remember?"

"So did I!" Hugh called.

"Me too!" Dennis laughed.

"Anyone else?" Kathy called in disbelief. "How many of you have become ordained ministers over the internet?" She looked around the room and three more hands shot up, and a fourth went up sheepishly, laughing.

Bruce and Rita hugged.

"Well, Rita, which one of these many qualified men and women would you like to perform our wedding services next week?"

"Oh Bruce, you choose!" she called.

The crowd of friends gathered around to offer congratulatory hugs and handshakes. Bruce put his arm around Rita and told her through the crowd, "I knew you'd be back."

With tears in her eyes, she spoke softly back to him. "I know."

ꕥ
~~~

Brian

By Bruce Nickerson

I flopped down next to Brian, "Sup?"

"Nothing." He was sitting on a somewhat tatty sofa on the sidewalk in front of "Stuff," a Good Will-like store. Not sure whether the sofa was waiting for trash pickup or to be sold by "Stuff."

"How was your weekend?"

"Not so good."

"On a day like this you say 'not so good?'" It was a beautiful sunny day: clear blue skies, crisp dry air, the kind of day that is one of the reasons people live in the Boson area.

Maybe in his late forties, an incipient pot belly, pleasant manner, Brian and I had an easy going, joking relationship. A "graduate" of the Wednesday group, he kept coming back for it. Said he enjoyed it. "No accounting for taste," I told him.

"Tell me about it. Your weekend."

"Actually it sucked."

"And?"

"Well…" and his voice trailed off. "I'm worried about Donna." Donna was a close friend of his from the group. She was much younger than Brian, had two kids.

"Nah, just friends," Brian responded when I quizzed him about their relationship. "Besides, didn't you say no sex for the first year's a good idea?" Some AA advice.

"That's changed," I responded. "First year you can have as much sex as you want. The next year you can have it with someone else." A fleeting smirk from Brian.

"Well what?" I asked after the comic relief allowed him time to get his head together. His face changed from a worried-about-Donna look, to something else. No longer the smile I sat down next to. "Brian, from your mouth to my ears."

"I slipped over the weekend." I suspected it wasn't Donna.

"Serious?"

"Serious enough that I seen my shrink every day since then, and gone to so many meetings I lost count."

"That bad?"

"Scared the shit out of me."

"How so?"

In a serious tone: "You know me—it's always been pills. Any kind. Put 'em down in front of me and they're in my throat before I can ask what they are."

"Yeah, I remember you saying that."

"Anything. You put it there I'll put it in my mouth not even knowing what it is."

"So. What'd you do this time? OCs, percs, Klonopin?"

"It wasn't pills. That's what scared me. When I was active, it was pills. Only pills. Never booze. Maybe on a hot day if someone gave me a cold one, I'd pop it open have a few swigs, get busy and forget it was there. No booze."

"And?"

"So I had it licked, right? No pills for a year. Clean. Feeling good."

I began to hear where he was going.

"Saw some friends in the square. They were just sitting there, looking straight. They had a few beers they were nursing from some paper bags. So I sat down to chat."

"Ah!"

"Next I know there's a paper bag in my hand with a beer inside and the beer is trickling down my throat. Don't remember anything else till next morning when I woke up in a bed with the worst head I ever had in my life. And scared shitless. Called my sponsor. He came over, we went to a noon meeting, and ever since then I been going to a meeting or seeing my shrink." Painful to be sitting close to someone you like, a grown man, and seeing him begin to cry.

"So, you coming to the meeting?"

"Yeah, but I gotta leave early to see my shrink again."

A few weeks later I was driving to the Wednesday meeting and saw Donna walking on the sidewalk. I pulled my car over, waited for her to catch up, hoping she wouldn't think me the neighborhood pervert. I rolled the car's passenger side window down and called out, "Hey Donna." She stopped.

"I thought that was your car," she said with her usual smile.

I leaned over to the open window. "Beautiful day." Another of those beautiful nowhere-but-Boston summer days. Donna walked over and leaned her head in the open window, her dark eyes smiling. "How you been?" I asked.

"Great."

"And the apartment?"

"It's good. I told you where it is, right?" She had. The building was a four family, two up and two down, that had just been rehabbed, repainted outside, and looked beautiful.

"Yeah. Looks real nice."

"It is."

"You have the kids over much?"

"Just began unsupervised visits last Saturday," she beamed. "Hope to get custody again."

"Hope so. Hey, I saw Brian last week and he said he hadn't seen you for a while. He was worried."

"Well, I haven't been to meetings for a while, haven't felt too well."

"Yeah, he said that. He hoped you were doing good though. You still going to OAS?" (Out Patient Addiction Services—a local hospital program for people in early recovery.) "Saw you walking in that direction."

"Nah, just an appointment with my shrink."

"Well, I'll let you go then. Nice day for a walk. I'll tell Brian I talked with you."

"OK. Was good talking. See you later."

I didn't. Neither did Brian.

ꟷ

Winston and Cassidy

By Jennifer Klein

Cassidy gently nudged open the door a few inches and peeked in. "Oh, goody. He's still sleeping," she stage-whispered to herself.

Carrying a breakfast tray, she tiptoed over the white carpet to her husband's sleeping body. He lay stretched on his back with his arm over his eyes. His chest rose and fell as he gently snored. She watched his white mustache hairs flicker with each breath. "Winston, darling," she sang.

He moved his arm from his eyes, but continued snoring.

"Winston, dear, are you going to make me eat all of this breakfast by myself?"

He snorted as he woke, jerking his body up with a start. "Wuh?"

"Winston, darling. I made your favorite! Huevos rancheros, with strawberries on the side, a glass of our own Florida orange juice and coffee."

He smiled, with eyes half open, and laughed a hoarse laugh. "You're just trying to butter me up."

"Now darling, don't be silly. Why on earth would I need to do that?"

"You know why. But, I'll take it." He sat up, fluffed the stack of white pillows behind him and took a sip of his black coffee. "Delicious. I could get used to this."

Cassidy laughed, smoothing her apron, which she kept on not because she needed it anymore, but because it looked festive to her, navy blue decorated with vibrant oranges, some whole and round, and some sliced so that their triangular sections came together in a juicy circle. It made her thirsty just thinking about those oranges, so thirsty that she had drunk four juice glasses of orange juice downstairs, along with a few strawberries and her usual scrambled eggs. She was not a big fan of huevos rancheros herself, she just wanted to surprise Winston since tomorrow they were going to start bright and early on a new adventure, and she didn't think he was so excited about this one.

"Bring your tray down when you've finished," she told him. She went downstairs to finish straightening up the kitchen. They were leaving tomorrow, and she had a lot of work to do.

After a few minutes, Winston came down the stairs, carrying his tray. "You sure we have to do this one?"

Cassidy was wiping the white marble counter with a damp cloth. "I think it will be good. Not the best but good." She stood next to him as he filled the sink with enough water to rinse his dishes. She removed the dishes from his tray and wiped the tray with a towel.

"Nothing could be better than the best." He smiled.

She laughed, grabbed his neck, and pulled him toward her for a kiss. "Thanks, darlin'." Her face flushed remembering. "But it'll be great."

He ran the scrub brush over his dishes in the sink and then placed them in the dishwasher.

Cassidy checked her apron for crumbs, then untied it and hung it neatly on its hook beside the pantry. "Are you going to work on your woodworking now?" She smoothed out her blue exercise suit, feeling her tummy underneath. She was heavier than she wanted to be, but who wasn't? She was exercising—keeping her bones strong, and staying healthy. Most importantly she was happy.

"In just a minute," Winston answered.

"What are you working on now?"

"Chairs! Some Shaker-style chairs in cherry. They're beauties."

"Sounds lovely. Would you mind taking the trash on the way out? I'm going to do a little run-walk."

He nodded, and she gave him a quick peck on her way out.

~~~

The phone rang as Cassidy stepped through her front door, returning from her walk. She could hear the sander buzzing in the garage. Winston would not be able to hear the phone. She ran through the entryway and into the kitchen to check the phone on the desk. It was Julie. She picked it up.

"Hellooo?" she sang into the phone excitedly.

"Mom! How are you?" She heard her daughter's voice on the other end.

"Wonderful, darling. And you? Would you like me to get your father? He's working on a chair in the garage."

"Oh don't bother. I just wanted to tell you guys to have fun tonight. And be careful. You know. Make sure to wear your wallet in your front pocket and all—or don't bring one at all."

"Of course, dear. I taught *you* that." She laughed.

"And how are you today?"

"We're fine. Winnie has been having a bit of a meltdown today. You know, we're still working on being nice. But Owen is Owen. He's doing his own thing. Today that means steering clear of Winnie."

"You went through the same mean streak when you were four. She'll grow out of it."

"I hope you're right. It's hard to figure her out. But we're having a bit of a heat wave up here, so Greg's planned a scooting outing at the park. Winnie always does best when she's playing outside."

"And how's Owen doing on his scooter?"

"He's got knee pads now, so at least he won't get so scraped up. He's coming along. Slowly, but he's getting it. Listen, Greg's getting the kids ready, so I'd better get going. But I hope you have a wonderful time!"
~~~

"Of course, dear! You too! I love you, honey. And give everyone my love."

"Love you too, Mom! And tell Dad I said to *have fun*!"

"Ok now!"

Cassidy remembered the day Winnie was born. Julie had called at seven a.m. to tell her parents the surprise news that the baby had arrived two weeks early, after a labor that started at two a.m. and lasted the rest of the night. Cassidy passed the phone to Winston so Julie could surprise her dad with a piece of the happy news herself.

"Congratulations on your new little girl!" he bellowed happily into the phone. "I can't believe we have two granddaughters now!" Justin and Sarah had had a little girl the year before. "And what's her name?"

She saw Winston laugh with delight. "You've named her Winnie! Is that Winifred? After me! Oh, little girl! I'm delighted! You've made my heart sing! Does she look like me?" He paused, "I guess it is too early to tell. Well, you probably need to get some rest. Your mom and I will buy the plane tickets today. We'll be out tonight or tomorrow. Congratulations, dear! I'm delighted. And honored!"

When Winston got off the phone, Cassidy saw him still smiling, his eyes shiny with tears. "They've named their little girl after me!"

"I know dear." She pulled him close to her in a hug.

"Little Winnie." He paused and then laughed. "Should I be offended that they named a girl after me?"

"Winston!" She elbowed him playfully.

"Well. They could have waited until they had a boy."

She laughed. "Well Winnie is such a great name. Winston, you know...is a little formal."

"True," he said laughing.

~~~

The next morning, as they were getting ready to leave for their latest adventure, Cassidy slipped her black Birkenstocks on and admired her orange toenails. Then she stood back and looked in the mirror. She smiled. She had on a full-length orange-flowered hippy skirt, a lovely white top and she had done her hair in tiny pigtails under a beautiful orange bandana. She looked like a hippie grandmother. Well, maybe a hippie grandmother with enough money to buy beautiful clothes.
~~~

Winston came out of the bathroom. "Cassidy, you are a vision!" He stood in front of her and slowly leaned forward, kissing her softly on the lips. She wrapped her arms around him.

"Why thank you, Winston." She looked up into his eyes and smiled. She released him and stepped back. "You don't look so bad yourself." Winston was wearing a new pair of baggy tan corduroys and a gray polo shirt. He had agreed to wear the corduroys, but there was no taking this man out of his polo shirts. He put foot powder in his boat shoes and slipped them on.

"Shall we?" he asked. They headed downstairs to the car.

"Have you got everything?"

"Everything, except an escape plan," he joked as he held the door open.

"Oh Winston, we'll be fine."

~~~

Their adventure days had started ten years ago, the day after their youngest, Derek, had left to study chemistry at Northwestern, Winston's alma mater. Cassidy would never forget it; she had lain in bed with Winston, this was before they had moved from Chicago to Florida, and they had both marveled how they had the house to themselves.

"I can't believe we did it," she said, curling up next to his warm tee-shirted chest. His arm was under her neck and he was facing her. "We have three beautiful children, and now they're out in the world."

He smiled back at her. "I can't believe we have the house to ourselves."

She drew in a deep breath and felt her heart pound and her mind flood with relief. They had done it. They had gone through Julie's whining stage, through Justin's impulsive stage, through Julie and Derek's know-it-all stages. They had made it through Julie's high school dating, and through Justin's playing-the-field stage, and through Derek's why-can't-I-get-a-date stage, and they had come out of it all whole and happy. Julie was in graduate school and dating someone they loved, Justin had a great job and had found the girl of his dreams (and theirs), and Derek was starting Northwestern, having finished fourth in his high school class.

"What are we going to do with ourselves?" she asked Winston with laughing eyes.
~~~

"I am going to have more time for my woodworking."

She laughed and buried her head under the covers.

"What?" He laughed, pulling the white down comforter off of her head. Her face and ears felt hot with embarrassment. "Why are you blushing?" he asked. His eyebrow arched.

"I have an idea," she mumbled.

"What kind of idea?" He was so handsome when he smiled, especially when he was smiling at her. His black hair was now more white than black and his mustache was nearly all white. Still, his lips were full and pink and his eyes were so bright and alive.

She buried her head back under the covers. "An adventure."

"An adventure?" he asked, trying to pull the covers back again, but Cassidy held them tight. "I can barely understand you. Why are you hiding under the covers?"

"A naughty adventure," she said, muffled from under the covers.

"A naughty adventure? What on earth are you saying under there?"

She poked her head out again. "We have the house to ourselves, right?"

"Right," he said.

"Let's start a mission."

"What kind of a mission?" A flicker of fear twitched over his face.

With her daring eyes, Cassidy looked at Winston, hesitated for a second, but then blurted out at record speed, "Let's start a mission to have sex in every room of the house." She threw the covers back over her head and held them down as tight as she could.

She waited a moment and then peeked out over the top of the covers. Winston was staring ahead with a bit of a silly grin on his face.

"Winston?" Maybe he would think she was crazy. Maybe he wouldn't want to see her old saggy body throughout the house. Maybe the glory days had been having the kids and they would be just another couple who lived for their grandkids. Who was she kidding? She was fifty-two, after all. But for goodness sake, on *Law and Order* and *House*, all of the old people behaved worse than sex-crazed teenagers—without a care in the world. Then there was *Cocoon*. When had she seen that movie? She must have been twenty-eight watching Hume Cronyn and Jessica Tandy getting together, when they were how old? Seventy? But man, Jessica Tandy, what a beautiful woman—and Hume Cronyn—he was beautiful too. Maybe, Cassidy thought, maybe she was just too wrinkled and saggy. Maybe if she got in shape. "Winston?" she asked again.

"When can we start?" he asked, still grinning sillily.

And so they did start. Nervously at first, and only in the dark, and on beds, couches and floors. But eventually Cassidy found herself surreptitiously suggesting that they "make love" in the kitchen the way that they had in some steamy junk novel she had read so long ago, or she would have Winston sneak in while she was having a bubble bath the way they had in some naughty teenage "romance" that she had snuck into her parent's house as a teenager. Of course she never told Winston that her ideas were coming from some novel or other that may actually still be hidden in the basement somewhere. It wasn't long before Winston himself began suggesting that they try out positions described in this episode of *Criminal Intent*, or shown in some episode of *Sex in the City*. And so they made it through all of the rooms. Against the running washing machine in the laundry room, bent over the office desk (*Criminal Intent* style), squished together in the dark coat closet, on the pool table in the basement, in the front entryway right after work (with trench coats, both).

And after a few months, they had actually done it. They had had sex in each room. Winston laughed out loud one day as they sat cuddling close, watching a movie, and as though it had just occurred to him, he announced, "Cassidy! We never 'did it' outside."

So one dark Friday night, they were in the process of fulfilling the final goal of their naughty adventure, when they saw some headlights pull in the driveway. Derek was home for a surprise weekend visit. Cassidy had never imagined two naked fifty-somethings could run so fast. They flashed down the upstairs hallway, Cassidy in the lead and Winston close behind, just as Derek had his key in the door. In their haste they slammed their bedroom door shut. Then they near about died laughing, although they kept as quiet as they could manage. Cassidy pretended to be sick and crabby as soon as she was able to pull herself together, and Winston got dressed as quickly as he could to bring everything back to normal, and welcome their son home.

~~~

This upcoming adventure was not quite so wild. Most of them weren't. Cassidy wasn't a fast woman after all. She had just wanted
~~~

some quality time with her husband after twenty-eight years of hard work raising a family. Well, they had continued watching a little *Sex in the City*, and even some naughty television on Cinemax and occasionally they would try out some new things they had learned from those shows, but they had happily accepted that as the new normal. On other adventures, they had hiked the narrows of Zion National Park, which had been a dream of theirs from the early days of their marriage. They had also run a half-marathon together. They had started a bowling league. Winston was a wonderful bowler, but as hard as she tried, Cassidy could never quite get the hang of it, although she did keep it up for two years. They had joined a tennis club with much more success, and they had even studied some ballroom dancing. Winston had suggested that they try to score some "dirty points"—something he remembered some guys talking about in his college days, but when they looked into that, they found out they would have to have sex in public places. For goodness sake, Cassidy thought, she volunteered at the library. She wasn't about to seduce her husband there.

~~~

After the long drive to their latest adventure, they finally pulled into the coliseum parking lot. There were hundreds of cars already there, and hundreds more were waiting in line to be directed to park. A family of four was unloading their car in the parking space right beside them. The father was pulling their tent out of the trunk as their preschool-aged daughter danced beside him. The mother slipped her young baby into a sling and smiled at Cassidy. Cassidy smiled back.

"See, Winston, It'll be alright."

"Well, just in case, Cassidy, I have to tell you. I scored some 'E.'"

"Oh Winston. Ecstasy? You're kidding."

"Well, I wish I weren't, Cassidy. Staying overnight at a Phish concert has me a little nervous."

"We'll be fine Winston. It's just Jam music."

"I know. I know." He laughed. "But maybe we can work on that 'E' as our next adventure."

"Winston!" She laughed, and then her smile stretched wide as she considered the possibility.
~~~

"Oh! I knew you were crazy, woman!" He closed his car door and met her by the trunk. "And that's why I love you."

ജ൫

8

WOMEN

Maggie After Dark

By Charlotte Christen

"I'll be home before dark," Maggie had said. But she wasn't, not dark on that day nor on the next. It was surprisingly easy to disappear. She hadn't done any planning, it just happened.

At first her husband was too embarrassed to admit to anyone, especially to the police, that she had not come home. By the time he did report her missing, a week later, Maggie had emptied her bank account, contacted her broker, cashed out her stocks and driven to the next state where she sold her car and bought a new one. The new car was unlike what anyone would ever imagine her to be driving. Good old predictable Maggie; surely she would drive a mushroom-colored Ford Sedan, not the custom painted purple Porsche 944 she selected off the used car lot from the dealer who seemed as eager to sell it to her as she was to buy it. She remembered how he kept looking over his shoulder and she'd wondered if maybe it had belonged to an ex-wife or girlfriend. He'd explained to her that most people buying a Porsche wanted a manual shift car and not a three speed automatic like the purple one she was looking at. It was still pricey, despite being used and apparently not what most buyers wanted.

Maggie also had her hair cut and dyed. Black. Mousey-brown long-haired Maggie was transformed into a black-haired Maggie with a short fringy modern cut. She'd always wanted black hair that would turn to white when she aged as her grandmother's had done. Of course, a dye job wouldn't alter her own hair's genetic color progression. She was fairly certain hers would only become a mousier brown streaked with gray; still, she enjoyed living with the illusion.

~~~

Twenty years passed quickly. Now here she was sitting in front of her old house in her former town in her latest car, a sedate metallic gray Ford Fiesta. It almost matched her hair as it was now, except for the metallic part. The house had been renovated by a new owner who added a brick patio on the side, a garden shed and an attached garage. A coat of pale yellow paint covered the white it was when Maggie last saw it. The original footprint appeared to be the same and she wondered if inside anything was as it had been twenty years ago.

Maggie studied the shrubbery for a long time; the Spirea or Bridal Wreath bushes she'd planted as a border between their house and the neighbors before she left were now many times larger, grown to privacy-fence height. In bloom now they were a dense row of graceful white blossoms. The new owners knew how to prune. The branches swooped gracefully to the ground, each one swathed with quarter-sized multi-floral heads that looked like miniature bridal bouquets. She had a desire to jump out of her car and rush over to pick a large armful, find a suitable vase and set them in the center of the dining room table on her grandmother's lace tablecloth. It's what she would do if she still lived in that house. She wondered if there was such a bouquet of flowers on that dining room table now. Maybe there wasn't even a dining room anymore. The latest style in houses like this was to take down walls to create family rooms by combining the formal dining room space with the kitchen or living room.
~~~

Maggie decided it would not be wise to either pick a bouquet or peek in the window to see about the dining room. Besides, if she did pick the flowers where would she put them? Her hotel room didn't have a suitable table, and furthermore, the flowers were lovely when fresh, but soon the tiny petals, along with the soft yellow pollen, would drop off, leaving a mess. Better the flowers stay on the shrub.

Maggie wondered if maybe she should take a picture of the house to keep as a memory of how it looked now after twenty years, but then she had no photos to remember how it had been. The house looked pretty good. She wondered if she looked as good after so long a time.

Leaving seemed so significant back then, so necessary. She loved her husband and daughter, her house, her life, her job, even her dog; but it wasn't satisfying. Her leave-taking had more to do with Maggie than with her family. The person she'd thought of as Maggie was disappearing, shrinking ever smaller and smaller until she was less and less the person she had been when she graduated from college. She was disappearing, soon she would be gone, invisible. The only solution she saw, the only way to save that self, was to get away. Nobody was to blame. Maggie herself had allowed it to happen. Somewhere in that pleasant life she stopped growing and began to blend into the background like the floral curtains hanging next to the floral wallpaper. She'd tried to help herself by enrolling in a class at the university. There she found other women feeling just as she did. By mid-term, Maggie was on the road in her purple car heading west.

When she reached Indiana she'd stopped at a wayside to eat lunch. She'd spread out her road map on the top of the picnic table to look for a town with an interesting name. There it was...Paris! And Paris was where Maggie went and where she had lived the past twenty years. She'd found a small apartment and a job as a waitress in the "Wholesome Paris Diner" on Main Street. There she became known as the woman who was always so nice and never asked questions, but when you talked to her, she listened. Maggie never offered advice, and when she left work, the customers and the diner remained behind. For twenty years Maggie worked, read, wrote in her journal and went to the movies at least once a week where she always bought the buttered popcorn.

Maggie's apartment had not changed during her sojourn in Paris. When she first moved in, she painted the walls in full rich earth colors, deep and vibrant golds, greens and red clay. She put a few framed movie posters on the walls. The furniture she bought was Shaker simple and on the floor she laid out several colorful Scandinavian rugs. That was it, surfaces were uncluttered, no photographs or mementos.

Maggie worked and Maggie kept to herself. Easy to do in Paris, Indiana. She never looked or thought back to what once was. With only herself to care for, she was always caught up with things that needed to be done. There was no long "To Do" list attached to her refrigerator door. For the first time in her life, Maggie had everything in control. For twenty years she lived that way.

Gradually during those years, Maggie had tired of driving two towns over to have her hair dyed and fringed, so she let it return to its natural color and grow longer. She tired of the attention drawn to her purple Porsche and sold it to a kid in his late teens who added his own creative designs to the purple paint work.

Then one day about a fortnight ago she felt she needed to see her old house and scheduled a two-week vacation. Now here she was sitting in front of her former life.

Maggie was startled to attention by somebody knocking on the car window. She lowered the pane and a young woman asked if she was all right.

"You've been sitting out here looking at my house for a long time," she said. "I've been watching you from the window of my study. Do you need anything? Are you lost?"

Maggie explained that once many years ago she'd lived in that house and was just stopping to look at it.

"Come on in for a cup of tea. I just brewed a pot. I'll show you around the inside and you can tell me if you like how it's changed."

Maggie followed the young woman up to the porch and in through the front door. Everything was different. The wallpaper was all gone and brilliant colors of a morning sunrise filled the rooms. Books lined all the walls.

"I'm a writer," the woman explained. "I bought this house about five years ago, shortly after my Dad died. When I was a kid we used to drive past here and he always said that it looked to him like a place where somebody might find happiness. I've made some changes as you can see. It's perfect for me and my cats."

They sat down for tea in the large kitchen, at the round antique oak pedestal table covered with a brightly colored cloth that appeared to be hand woven. In the center of the table was a large bouquet of Bridal Wreath just beginning to drop its petals and pollen.

ꕥ

Schenectady Biplane

By Alma Hart

(From the prompt of a picture from the Empire State Aerosciences Museum, Schenectady, New York, showing a woman with her biplane.)

I keep this picture of my great-grandmother on my desk for inspiration.

They had no children yet, so there was no challenge for her in her little house, especially when he traveled. She just didn't admire the silverware enough to polish it. She had always been a daddy's girl, Lou not Louise, who would rather help her father at the factory than her mother at home. Once she had bobbed her hair there was no going back.

Anyway, this is the story my Dad told me about why he calls me Lou not Lu-Lu. She had read about the planes being experimented with nearby while Great-Grandpa Ted was away for a few weeks on important business. So, she decided to spend a big part of her inheritance to invest in a biplane. She imagined making money delivering things to the rural areas of Wisconsin and Indiana. She let the local paper write a front page story on her because it would be good for her business plans.

She forgot that it might be bad for her marriage when her husband saw it. The ticket guy at the station showed him the article as soon as he stepped off the train. It was dark, he was tired, and there was his wife on the front page of the weekly, posing next to an airplane. He said that that was when he abandoned any hope of ever coming home to a hot meal cooked just for him. But, he was an easygoing guy who had married that hoyden heiress because she was adventuresome enough for both of them.

She flew the plane delivering supplies to farms for a quite a few years until the stock market crashed and she had to sell it to support Great-Grandpa's machine parts business. She was always angry that it wasn't a crash of hers that took her out of the sky. But then she found new adventure raising four boys and my grandmother, Sarah, the spitfire. But that's another story.

ꙮ

Jeanette and the Invitation

By Rhona Barlevy

Jeanette approached the mailbox with great trepidation. She just knew the invitation would be there. The envelope, probably crisp and white with great gold embellishments, her name and the return address in a flourish of calligraphy that would be elegant and not overstated. Nancy had always had a gift for presentation. Jeanette sighed as she pulled the door open to the mailbox and peaked inside it. Yup, there it was, gold trim and all, leering out from under her telephone bill and a reminder post card from the dentist. She pulled the door fully open and removed the mail, managing somehow in the process to drop all but the invitation in the dirt below the mailbox. Jeanette could feel herself growing unbearably irritable as she bent down to retrieve the mail.

"Damn," she yelled with more anger then the situation warranted. The hot sweaty flush that rose up from inside her made every little dissonant sound unbearable, her skin so prickly that even the touch of clothing on her body felt agonizing. She hated that she could not control it. Tears rose up in her eyes as she shook the dirt from the mail.

"Fuck Nancy and this whole stupid wedding," she yelled as she slammed the door of the mailbox shut.

Jeanette stomped into the house. She threw the mail on the already cluttered table in the entryway and headed for the kitchen where she frantically looked around for something to eat. Grabbing the first thing she could find, a stale onion bagel, she stuffed it into her mouth. She chewed hard and rapidly, ripping new pieces fiercely from the vitrified cardboard-textured object in her hand. Jeanette's jaw began to ache and tighten from the effort, but she could feel the blessed relief of her body relaxing and the torturous sensitivity ebbing. In fact, an intense weariness began to descend over her, and as she swallowed the last mouthful, she crumpled into the closest kitchen chair. She was not particularly happy at how she had handled her irrational state, but at least now she felt in control again.

She and Nancy had been roommates through four years of college, and the relationship had been a conflicted one for Jeanette. She had spent many hours then, as she frequently did now, comparing herself to Nancy. Tall, willowy, bright, and talented, Nancy always achieved whatever she set her mind to, which now was a rocketing career as director of marketing for a national food corporation, and soon, marriage to a very handsome and prominent New York financier. The most irksome part was that Jeanette actually liked Nancy. She was fun and funny, generous, creative and upbeat. Nancy did have a tendency towards self-promotion and proclamation, but Jeanette found it to be a small flaw given her other attributes. What she really envied most was Nancy's ability to handle a crisis and roll with the punches. Everything was such a struggle for Jeanette. Constantly saturated with anxiety, she always expected the worst and was repeatedly second guessing her abilities. She had never genuinely gone after what she wanted, invariably starting toward things but never finishing them. She often settled for what came, and then spent her time regretting her choices.

Jeanette was deep into her miserable ruminating when she was suddenly startled by the sound of the front door banging shut. A minute later, her husband Ron stood in the doorway of the kitchen, the loathed invitation in his hand.

"Hey did you see this, babe? It's the invitation to Nancy's wedding. Nice envelope huh, should be quite the shindig. How long has it been since we've seen her? About two years?"

Jeanette looked up at him and could feel her ever lurking irritability begin to rise again. God, couldn't he just shut up for once she thought - yap yap yap - like some hyperactive terrier.

"Yes I saw the invitation Ron," she said in the slow stilted way you might talk to someone mentally challenged. "Yes it is very nice, and it's been almost three years since we've seen Nancy."

"Oh really, well time flies I guess," he said as he dropped the envelope on the table while removing his tie with his other hand. "She's a great gal," Ron continued. "It should be a fun weekend in New York. So what's for dinner?"

Jeanette decided to ignore the first half of Ron's comment and just address the dinner issue. "Well I don't know, I just got home myself and I'm kind of tired and don't particularly feel like cooking."

"So no biggy, we could do take out, what would you like?" he responded affably.

What I would like, thought Jeanette, is someone who would come home, notice I'm tired or upset, and actually have an adult conversation with me about my day. But instead she wearily responded, "Whatever, I'm not very hungry, so get what you want and I'll find something in the frig."

"Okay, then I'll do a beer run and pick up a pizza. Could you call Romero's and order an everything pizza with extra cheese? I'm going upstairs to change," Ron said as he exited the kitchen. Jeanette watched Ron's stocky body amble down the hallway and once again felt the heavy regret of settling for what came.

Over the next several days, Jeanette was obsessed with finding an excuse not to attend Nancy's wedding. She whispered them to herself at work and spoke them out loud at home, but nothing sounded right, none of the reasons seemed plausible. One evening as the deadline to respond to the invitation grew near, Jeanette stood at the kitchen counter cutting up vegetables for dinner and stuffing potato chips in her mouth. She rhythmically chopped and chewed and in very short order, to her astonishment, the bag of chips was empty.

"Just great," she thought disgusted. "Now if I go to the wedding I'll be even fatter and dumpier, and I have absolutely nothing that fits. Then I'll have to go shopping, which I hate, and end up buying something I know I'll never wear again. This just gets better and better." While Jeanette was vehemently throwing the depleted bag into the trash, the phone rang. "Ron," she yelled, "could you please answer that, I'm making dinner." No response. "Ron could you pleeeeease answer the phone?" she yelled. Then overhead she heard clomping footsteps and the shrill ringing stopped. Through the floorboards she could hear Ron's deep voice and laughter, it sounded as if he was flirting. Overcome with curiosity, Jeanette rinsed her hands, dried them on her apron and walked to the bottom of the staircase. "Hey Ron," she yelled up, "is that for me?" Again, no response. All Jeanette could hear was the continued rumblings of Ron's voice. "Ronnnnnnnnnn," she yelled, repeating louder, "is that for me?" Finally after a few more seconds of conversation he appeared at the top of the stairs.

"It's Nancy," he said with a smile that took up most of his face.

"Nancy?" Jeanette inquired.

"Yes," said Ron, with a hint of uncharacteristic sarcasm in his voice. "Nancy, you know, who lives in New York and is getting married next month? That Nancy."

"Oh," she responded, staring dumbfounded at Ron as he handed her the phone. Jeanette robotically brought the receiver to her ear and began to will herself to speak. "Hey Nance," she heard herself say in a bright animated voice that surely belonged to someone else. "I was just thinking of you and how much fun the wedding will be."

"Oh great," Nancy answered. "I'm glad you're coming, but that's not why I called. I'm going to be in Boston on business Friday and have a few unscheduled hours before my flight back. We haven't seen each other in ages so I thought maybe we could meet for an early dinner and catch up. It really has been a long time."

Jeanette continued in an overly perky voice. "What time did you have in mind?"

"How about 5:30 at the Boston Harbor Hotel?" said Nancy.

"The Boston Harbor Hotel!" Jeanette exclaimed, anxiously losing her perky cool.

"Don't worry. It's my treat," Nancy replied, giving a short laugh. "One of the perks of having an expense account."

"I guess it is. That's very nice of you, I've always wanted to go there," Jeanette said, regaining her composure. "So I'll see you at 5:30 on Friday."

~~~

"God these drivers are such morons," Jeanette muttered out loud as she sat in rush hour traffic. "That stupid Volvo's making a left—just go around on the right—can't you people figure out how to do that?" Her voice rose with anger and frustration as she castigated the drivers ahead of her in the intersection. "Damn, I'll never make this light," she continued, rapidly tapping the steering wheel as she spoke. "I don't know why I said yes to this, Friday night of all nights," she said as the cars inched forward. Finally an hour later, and amazingly only five minutes late, she arrived at the restaurant. Jeanette felt tarnished and frazzled as she entered the dining room, and she was certainly not ready to deal with Nancy. As she stood in the entry scanning the crowd for her friend, a flawlessly groomed and attired maître d' approached her. He stood with extremely erect posture and openly looked her up and down.
~~~

"May I help Madame?" he said with what Jeanette was certain was a sneer on his face.

Although she felt herself being rendered mute by his stare, she managed to stammer out, "I'm, I'm meeting a friend."

"And what name is the reservation under?" he asked in a clipped tone.

"Nancy Stanton," she squeaked in response. The maître d' walked over to a slim black metal stand and consulted a gold-trimmed red board with a sheet of paper on it.

"Well, Madame, I see the reservation, but Ms. Stanton has yet to arrive." He turned to face Jeanette, and continued. "Perhaps you could wait in the lounge and I will seat you both when she is present."

Feeling totally humiliated, Jeanette scurried off to the darkest corner of the lounge to await Nancy's arrival. She was in the midst of berating herself for letting that pompous maître d' get to her, when she noticed a tall blond in an impeccably tailored gray suit with a rose-colored silk blouse approaching the lounge. The woman was rail thin, her face all boney prominences and cadaverous hollows, but her blonde hair was a thick and perfectly coiffed chin length cap. Then, much to Jeanette's surprise, as the woman came closer, she realized it was Nancy. As she rose to greet her friend, she pinned on her other-person cheery face.

"Jeanette," Nancy called out as she grew closer, "hi, sorry I'm late, got caught with a last minute call I had to take. You know what it's like."

Well, no, I don't, thought Jeanette, but I'll pretend I do. "Oh that's okay Nancy, I know how it is, and you're not really late, I just got here myself." They gave each other an I'm-too-dressed-up-to-hug-you hug, and kissed the air on the side of each other's cheeks. After they were seated by the imperious maitre d', a staunchly dressed, prim and overly mannered waiter appeared and introduced himself as Walter, their server for the evening. Walter handed each of them a leather-bound menu with embossed gold lettering, and then began reciting, in a rather sing-song voice, the evening's dinner specials. As Jeanette watched this spectacle, she could feel a giggle bubbling up into her throat and had to force herself to look down at the menu to avoid laughing out loud. She had the strangest sensation that she was in a Monty Python skit.

Walter finished his specials' rendition and asked, "Are you ladies ready to order or shall I give you a few more moments?"

"No, I'm ready. How about you, Jeanette?" Nancy asked.

"Well why don't you order first, and by the time you're done I will be."

"Okay," said Nancy, and as she looked up at the waiter she smiled. "I'll have the goat cheese salad with dried cranberries and walnuts. I would like the goat cheese and the walnuts on the side, and please put only five cranberries in the salad. Oh, and please, no dressing, just some lemon wedges, also on the side."

Walter diligently wrote every detail and then asked, "What would Madam care to drink?"

"Well," responded Nancy, "I'll have some sparkling water. Do you have Badoit?"

"Yes we do, and might I add that's an excellent choice." Then, with a pinched smile, the waiter turned to Jeanette. "And what can I get for you, Miss?"

Jeanette, dumbfounded at Nancy's order, and feeling a little intimidated by the piercing stare of the waiter, just mumbled, "I'll have the broiled salmon with the reduced balsamic vinaigrette glaze, roasted vegetables and a glass of your house chardonnay."

When the waiter departed, Nancy smiled and said, "You know I would love to order some wine and salmon, but I need to watch every calorie. It's so competitive in New York you just can't afford to let yourself go."

Jeanette was so astonished at the remark that not even her perky other-person self could think of a reply. As she was struggling to come up with one, Walter returned with their drinks and set them down with almost militaristic precision.

"So, what have you been up to?" Nancy asked after the waiter had departed. "Still at the same job? What was that agency, some children's social services place or something?"

"Yes," said Jeanette. "I am."

Nancy's eyebrows arched in surprise, "Really? But you must be at least a supervisor or director by now?"

Jeanette felt a hot flush creeping up her chest and onto her face. She wasn't sure if she was more hurt or angry, and she certainly was confused as to whom this woman was who sat across the table. "Actually, I am not either Nancy, I prefer working directly with the kids and not sitting at some desk shuffling papers and refereeing staff conflicts." She realized as the words came out of her mouth that for the first time she was being someone with Nancy that she recognized.

"I guess that has its rewards," Nancy replied offhandedly, and then she launched into a broadcast of all her recent accomplishments and activities, including a blow-by-blow description of some new marketing ploy she developed for selling prepared frozen peanut butter and jelly sandwiches to busy career moms. After about fifteen minutes of her friend's bombastic barrage, Jeanette realized she was no longer able to pay attention, much less care about what was being said. She allowed her gaze to drift around the room with all its well-healed, fashionably attired patrons eating their artfully-arranged dinners in the tasteful décor of the dining room. Suddenly she had a great urge to be in MacDonald's gorging on a Big Mac while great gobs of ketchup dripped down the front of her Red Sox tee shirt.

"Jeanette, Jeanette are you okay?" Nancy asked, her voice sounding more annoyed then concerned as she leaned in closer.

Jeanette startled and, a little embarrassed at being caught in her musings, reddened. "Oh sorry Nance, I guess I drifted a little, it's been a long day and the wine seems to have made me a little sleepy."

"Will you be able to drive?" Nancy asked, leaning in closer scrutinizing Jeanette's face.

"Oh yeah, I'm sure after I eat I'll feel more energized."

Nancy, her concerns mollified, straightened in her chair and launched right back into her discourse. "Well as I was saying, Alan and I are looking for another apartment, preferably on the upper east side, we need something to accommodate office space at home, and large enough for entertaining. We've ended up having to look in the two and a half mil range as we just can't get the kind of amenities we want for under that in Manhattan."

Jeanette, stunned at this, asked, "What sort of amenities do you need that cost that much?"

"Well," said Nancy, reaching into her oversized Gucci bag and pulling out her iPhone. "Here are photos of some places we are considering. As you can see they have well-appointed kitchens, with all the latest appliances and gadgetry. And we really need a state-of-the-art kitchen."

"Really, Nance, I didn't know you were so into cooking," Jeanette said, her head spinning from the parade of industrial strength, sterile chrome and granite kitchens Nancy rapidly produced before her on the phone's small screen.

"Oh, I don't cook at all. Who has time, working the hours I do, but a good kitchen will be important for resale, and of course for the caterers to use when we entertain."

Plus, Jeanette thought, how else could we impress the hell out of everyone?

Fortunately, this painful conversation was interrupted with the arrival of their entrees. Jeanette stared incredulously at the plate placed before Nancy. The meal looked like it would be more at home in a hamster cage then on a dining table. She sighed sadly and then looked down at her own plate with the staged arrangement of vegetables surrounding the salmon. On top was drizzled a thin swirling line of sauce that Jeanette knew would not be sufficient to disguise the taste of what smelled like not so fresh fish. She could feel the muscles in her neck tighten, her head starting to pound, and the air in the room was becoming stifling and hot. As Jeanette began to eat her meal, a bilious nausea kicked up in her stomach and she regretted the wine she had drunk. Gratefully, the conversation for the remainder of the meal was banal, focusing on which old college chums would be at the wedding, and Jeanette managed to hold it together.

"So," Nancy said as she finished her coffee, black with half a Sweet and Low, "I guess I'll see you in a few weeks?" Jeanette smiled back weakly and prayed her dinner would stay down.

A few minutes later, after saying a hurried goodbye, Jeanette rushed out of the restaurant and found herself on the Boston Harbor boardwalk behind the hotel. She began rapidly gulping the cool night air to ward off the rising nausea that had plagued her throughout the meal. Slowly, her head cleared, her stomach settled and she began to grow calmer, relieved to finally be free of Nancy and the suffocating restaurant. She stood watching the few boats out at that hour as they silently sliced through the ripples of the current, their lights reflecting in squiggly patterns on the water. A deep rumbling boat horn could be heard in the distance, and as some of the moored boats rocked in the current, a musical clanging could be heard from the looser metal sail parts. The early October air was fragrant with the spicy scent of salt water and an underlying crisp fall perfume. She began to feel at peace, as if the currents of the harbor were washing through her and cleaning out all the flotsam and jetsam in her life. Somehow, this dreaded dinner with Nancy had turned into an epiphany. Jeanette laughed to think that Nancy had bragged so about her biggest accomplishment, a marketing campaign to sell pre-made peanut butter and jelly sandwiches. But it also saddened her to think that with all the promise, talent and intelligence Nancy had, she had chosen not to make more of a contribution with her life and now seemed just a shadow of her former self. It really put Jeanette's life in perspective. She occasionally made peanut butter and jelly sandwiches for her clients, but mostly she tried, and sometimes succeeded, in saving their lives. There was much in her life she loved, however, it seemed that her incessant discontent and disparaging negativity kept her from the pleasure of it. Look at how much time she had spent comparing herself to Nancy, envying her, and, in reality, she had been jealous of a ghost.

So, Jeanette thought, what am I going to do about all this craziness? She had tried therapy in the past, but it had been of little use, as she was never willing to accept her part in her own misery. Now she was, and that, as she always told her clients, made all the difference. "Time to practice what I preach," she said out loud. And with a smile on her face, and a decidedly lighter step, Jeanette began walking back to where she had parked her car. She realized she was looking forward to going home to her cozy little cape, with the funky, warm fifties kitchen resplendent with Formica counters, white appliances and a hot pink Naugahyde dinette set.

Forty five minutes later, she was parking her car in the driveway to her home. She locked the car door and turned to walk up the front path when she noticed that Ron had not put on the outdoor lights. Damn it, Ron, irritability beginning to rise up from her chest how hard could it be to remember to put on the lights? Jeanette stomped her way up the path, and just as she put her key in the lock she became aware that she was about to go inside and berate Ron yet again for some small infraction. Ron was a good guy; he didn't deserve to be treated this way. She leaned her head against the front door, and as small tears welled up, she realized how difficult the road ahead was going to be.

"But," Jeanette said softly, out loud, "I am going to do this, I am going to change." Then she took a deep breath, straightened herself, and stepped inside.

"Ron," she called as she walked down the hall.

"I'm in the back room watching the game," he responded.

Jeanette walked to the end of the hall and saw Ron seated in his black leather recliner with their orange tabby Tootsie curled up in his lap. Tootsie adored Ron and preferred his company over chasing mice, birds and eating treats. It seemed Ron knew all the right spots to scratch and all the fun games. Tootsie was purring so loudly Jeanette wondered how Ron could hear the sportscaster announce the game.

"So, how was dinner? That place is pretty pricey, I'm glad Nancy was paying."

"You know, it wasn't so great," she replied. "I felt uncomfortable with all that stupid formality, and the fish I ordered wasn't even fresh. We get better fish at that hole-in-the-wall dive we go to in Gloucester."

"I'm not surprised, you and I are more hamburgers at a diner type people."

Jeanette laughed. "Yeah we are and I'm glad of it. You know," she continued, "the whole thing was sort of an ah-ha moment for me. I've always been a bit jealous of Nancy and tonight I couldn't figure out why."

Ron's eyes raised in surprise as he said, "Really? I always thought you liked her. When I met you, the two of you were always gabbing and going places together."

"Yeah you're right we did," Jeanette said. "But that was quite a while ago. She isn't the same person anymore and I don't really like who she is now. She's all caught up in what's trendy and money and status. And she never stops talking about herself."

"Wow," he responded. "Are we going to go to the wedding?"

"Yeah," Jeanette said. "I think we should, there are some friends from college I would like to see, and we could use a really fun weekend away."

"That's fine with me." He was smiling from ear-to-ear. "But I have one question."

"What's that?" she said, smiling back.

"I'd like to know who you are and what you've done with Jeanette?!"

Jeanette laughed out loud and startled Tootsie who let out such a loud mournful meow that it made them both laugh. "Well I'm going to go upstairs and read in bed for a while," she said as she got up from her chair.

"Okay, the game is over in about half an hour, then Tootsie and I will be up too," Ron responded.

Jeanette left the room and stopped in the front hall to retrieve the invitation. As she ascended the stairs to the bedroom, she looked at the gilded envelope and was appalled that these pieces of paper had created such turmoil. And she was so ashamed at how she had been treating Ron. She didn't know where things would go, but maybe there was a chance to turn it around. She entered the bedroom and placed the invitation on her night stand. The response card would go out in the morning. Then she put on her favorite blue penguin pajamas, clicked on the lamp and, with book in hand, slid into bed. The cool crisp sheets further relaxed her as she lay back against the pillows, and for once in a long while, she looked forward to a good night's sleep and what possibilities the next day might bring.

ༀ

Thelma Checks Out

By Charlotte Christen

Whatever was expected of her, Thelma gave. She smiled when she was supposed to smile. She expressed joy when the situation called for it. When distain was warranted, Thelma expressed distain. When charities asked for money or her time, Thelma offered up her funds or the hours of her day. When Thelma's family wanted reassurance, she gave it to them; when her friends needed consolation, she was there for them; and when her husband wanted agreement with his ideas or decisions, she expressed that agreement. Thelma always gave it her all.

But, what about Thelma? What did she want or need? She didn't know. This came to her one day as she sat in the front parlor of her house, the same house where she had lived her entire life, the house that had been in her family for a hundred and fifty years. Thelma was looking out of the windows watching cars drive by. She watched people hurrying along the sidewalks en-route to events possibly of their own choosing. When had she last done that? Decide on her own what to do without input from others; to say it aloud and then actually do it? Thelma was no longer sure she knew what she wanted to do. She'd been so busily healing hurt feelings and keeping the peace for so many years that she knew the desires, wishes, pains and heartbreaks of her entire family more than she knew her own. Always wanting peace, Thelma knew exactly what to say or do in any situation to spread a healing balm over any injury, physical or emotional. Thelma had learned well the lessons of womanhood for her generation.

The tea kettle was whistling in the kitchen. She heard its piercing sound growing louder by the second.

"Thelma, I'm boiling, Thelma, I'm hot, Thelma, come make the tea, Thelma, Thelma, Thelma." That's what the tea kettle was screaming out to her.

She stayed where she was, in her chair by the window. It was easy to say no to a tea kettle. It had no questioning eyes, no puzzled expression, no angry face. So Thelma stayed where she was while the teapot screamed out for attention.

Thelma continued watching the cars and the people in front of her house. She watched the porch of the house kitty-corner across the street where the old woman, Dunnel, used to live. Dunnel who when Thelma was a small child still heated her kitchen with a wood stove and pumped water from a hand pump in her kitchen sink. Dunnel, who baked delicious cinnamon raisin coffeecakes and gave them away, coffeecakes that she remembered her father would refuse to eat. Why didn't he like Dunnel's coffeecakes, Thelma wondered. Maybe he didn't like Dunnel?

The whistling eventually grew quieter; she could hear a faint sputtering sound and then a scorching smell began to drift out of the kitchen. Thelma stayed where she was sitting, now watching the house directly across from the window where she sat. That's where Marjorie used to live, one of her friends who moved away long ago. She'd been a vivacious girl, always going out on dates. Thelma had envied her. Thelma still envied her.

The smell became stronger and must have drifted outside to summon her husband, James. She could hear the door slam and his footsteps pounding up the stairs to the kitchen.

"Thelma, for God's sake, the tea kettle. You've burned the bottom of another one. That's the third one now. Can't you pay attention to what you're doing?"

So, she'd done this before, Thelma thought. When she got to the kitchen, James had turned off the burner on the stove and was cooling off the bottom of the tea kettle under the faucet, the spigot turned on full force. All the creases in his face slanted downward with annoyance. Thelma apologized, saying she didn't know what came over her, she must have dozed off.

"I'll heat some water in a saucepan so we can have tea," she said, "and I'll stay right here to watch it. It won't happen again."

"How about some of those cookies I like with the tea, the ones you baked yesterday?" James replied, and Thelma got out a plate for James' favorite cookies, double chocolate chip. She didn't like chocolate but they were James' favorites. She would eat only one.

Thelma gave thought to her ditziness as James referred to it. It wasn't only the teapots; she knew that last tuna noodle casserole she'd cooked for the church supper was dreadful. There wasn't nearly enough tuna or even noodles to balance off the can of mushroom soup she'd mixed into it. The kitchen committee hadn't asked her since then to make anything. Thelma had known it wouldn't be good, but she'd taken it to the church supper anyhow. Perhaps she'd known that if it was bad they wouldn't bother her for another one. Besides, if she'd used up all the cans of tuna, she would have to go to the food market for more and Thelma had grown to hate shopping. It needed to be done over and over again, every week. It was like laundry; that too needed to be done every week. She'd begun wearing the same outfit every day to cut down on the amount of wash she would have to do. She liked the skirt and sweater she was wearing, her favorite black and white tweed skirt and a charcoal gray sweater, long sleeves. Even in the summer she liked to wear that sweater despite the heat. With the windows closed, the temperature easily climbed to eighty five degrees. When her children visited, they urged her to turn on the central air conditioning, but Thelma wouldn't do it. It was nicer warm.

James and Thelma sat down with their cups of tea and the cookies.

"Great cookies, Thelma. You sure know how to bake. Best I've ever eaten."

"Why, thank you, James," Thelma responded. She did not mention she'd purposely left out half of the chocolate chips. Nobody ever noticed small omissions, she'd decided. It saved money, too, if she used fewer chips. James was still happy and that's what was important.

Thelma was wishing they could go to the movies in the afternoon and for a drive over to the lake afterwards where they could stop for dinner at that little fish place on the shore near Darboy.

"I thought perhaps we'd go to Casey's Butcher Shop," James said. "Pick up some brats for supper. You can parboil them with onions in beer and I'll grill them. We'll invite Harry and Helen over and maybe play cards? Make some of that hot potato salad with the sweet and sour sauce to go with them and that apple cobbler we bake on the grill. How does that sound?"

"Good idea," Thelma responded. "I'll call Helen to invite them after we finish tea."

All her life Thelma had been passive about her wants and needs. She understood they were not identical, "wants" and "needs." She'd always had her "needs" satisfied, but somewhere along the timeline of life, her "wants" had disappeared into the Want Vat of everybody else's "wants," swirled into the soup, so-to-speak, and no longer discernible. For some time now, she'd been ignoring this discovery.

She would have fun with Helen and Harry. It would mean a lot of work for her before suppertime, but it would be fun. Yet, in Thelma's mind there was a niggling disturbance; it wasn't what she wanted to do today. She rarely got what she, Thelma, wanted. Everybody assumed that she would want what they wanted, hadn't it always been like that?

Thelma was coming to another conclusion. Those "wants" of hers were turning into "needs." If they were not looked to soon, and satisfied, something, she was not sure what, would surely transpire. This is where Thelma's wandering thoughts were taking her when she began to peel the potatoes for the salad.

Later, when the four of them sat outside at the picnic table, having finished eating the brats and potato salad, James said he'd go in to get the dessert to put on the grill while they played cards.

"Dessert?" Thelma queried. "What dessert?"

"You know, the apple cobbler we talked about when we were having tea? You said you were making it."

"Oh," Thelma responded, "I did? I guess I forgot. Well, maybe we can have some of those leftover chocolate chip cookies for dessert. Bring out a plate of them when you come back from the kitchen."

"But Thelma, I ate all of those this afternoon!"

"Well, James, bring out a box of crackers, those saltines will be just fine, right, Helen? Harry? You like saltine crackers, don't you? We can put some grape jelly on them."

In the end, they all decided to forgo dessert this time and just have a cup of decaffeinated coffee.

Thelma lost every hand at cards; why couldn't they play Scrabble once in a while, or that new word game her granddaughter brought over, the one in the banana-shaped canvas bag?

~~~

As days, months and years passed, Thelma became more and more impatient with people. Funny, she'd never before noticed how annoying they could be, always wanting to do things their way. And when her sister visited, why did she always talk so much? Couldn't she just shut up and enjoy the peace and quiet? Nothing she said was of any interest to Thelma anyhow. Who cared what she was reading? Then, too, she'd become rather fat, and so the next time Thelma saw her sister, she told her so right after she mentioned to her how much she disliked that blue dress she was wearing. Who did she think she was anyway, putting on airs, dressing up in that fancy dress to go out when Thelma was wearing her everyday skirt and sweater?

There were some things Thelma enjoyed. She liked to work in her garden and take walks around the neighborhood. The daily paper had crossword puzzles, and every day Thelma worked them with her ball point pen. Her sister couldn't do that. Thelma had always liked puzzles and she was good at them. Once a week she visited her cousin, Annie; she and James walked the eight blocks to Annie's house and back again. Sometimes they stayed for supper when Annie had cooked some recipe that had been in the family for years. They ate, did the dishes, exchanged news about other relatives, and Annie would show Thelma the projects she'd been working on, her crafts and crocheting. Thelma no longer did projects or crocheting, but she liked to see what Annie had made. Other times, though not as often, they drove across town to visit her elderly Aunt Maude and Uncle Cal who lived next to conservation land where Cal attracted many different types of birds to his bird feeders. Sometimes deer would wander into their yard and that too was exciting to watch. He had an illegal salt lick for them on his side of the conservation land border.

Then Annie died and the next year Aunt Maude died, too. Uncle Cal became cranky and was no longer fun to be around even with his yard full of birds and animals. Thelma had no one to visit. Maybe,
~~~

she thought, she should not have retired from her secretarial job as early as she had; maybe she should have worked harder to accept that new computerized system the bank installed. But she hadn't. Thelma had always been hesitant about trying or knowing anything new, be it foods, activities or people.

As her thoughts turned more and more to her "needed wants," Thelma started to remove herself from life as it had always been, consciously first and then she could no longer control it.

If she did not like or was not interested in what was being said, she stopped listening. It wasn't that she forgot what was said or what she was asked, she never heard it. At meal time she ate what was put on the table only if she wanted to eat it. If she didn't, she pushed it away. When James set out her pills in the morning, she would complain that he was trying to poison her and refuse even to take her vitamins. If a drive to visit someone was planned, she questioned repeatedly why they were going, and once there, when she wanted to return home, she would shout, "James, take me home now!"

Instead of Thelma adjusting to people in her life, people began to adjust to Thelma, and Thelma adjusted herself to routines. Breakfast every day followed the same pattern. Coffee, juice and cornflakes with a banana sliced on top; she carried these on a tray to the parlor where she sat, ate and looked out the window. The days of the week passed by like the colorful messages and pictures her aunts used to embroider on their dish towels: Monday/Washday, Tuesday/Ironing day, Wednesday/Baking day and so on through the week. Though she no longer performed any of these tasks, if asked, she would say she was still doing them.

Thelma's world closed in further as life's stimulating and varied experiences lessened. Her querulousness intensified as her reliance on each day's sameness grew.

After a time, Thelma no longer made a decision to let the tea kettle boil dry. When it whistled, she was unable to understand its message.

"Is that a parade going by the house?" she might say. "I hear a parade."

Thelma had checked out.

ജ്ജ

9

PEOPLE AND PLACES

Lucky

By Mindy Pollack-Fusi

Lucky. How attached she was to her Dalmatian for so many years. I can still remember my little girl, less than two years old, standing before all the stuffed animals stacked on a wall at Bloomingdales like pegs on a pegboard. Mel approached the display with arms outstretched and said, gently but repeatedly, "Hold, hold, hold." She knew enough not to grab the merchandise until Mommy or Aunt Marva gave permission. Aunt Marva, indeed, pounced on this opportunity to satisfy her niece by offering to pay the thirty-eight dollars that would make Lucky Mel's favorite friend from that day forth. At bedtime, she cuddled Lucky's black-speckled face so near to hers that the two seemed to smile over their close friendship. During the day, while Mel toddled off to daycare, Lucky sat atop her Little Mermaid pillowcase, proudly propped up beside Gore, a stuffed gorilla Dad bought her for his house, which she later carried home to mine.

When my little girl grew up, one day Lucky was relegated to a shelf high up on her bookcase. By then, Mel had real friends—and real canines, the three cocker spaniels that have passed through her life warming her bed many nights, sleeping beside her and Lucky. High up on the shelf, Lucky sat beside the other conglomeration of stuffed animals: a pink fabric dinosaur I'd bought her as an infant; the white floppy dog I gave an unexpected haircut when I tossed it cavalierly in the wash and drier, its long white hair now a tight poodle style; and the golden retriever that reminds me of the precious Holden who lived across the street at Mel's best friend's house.

One day, Mel and that best friend's relationship faded around the same time Lucky found his way to the shelf, with Mel moving on to new middle school friends that seemed to more aptly fit her rapid social maturity. So, too, Lucky was no longer required holding, as Mel developed crushes on boys, started attending dances, then proms, and soon had boyfriends who absorbed more of her time and devotion than Lucky ever did.

When she left for college five states away three autumns ago, I wondered if she developed a renewed need for Lucky. Would he comfort her at night while she slept near a stranger—a roommate she'd just met? Would he be a beacon to home when she felt lost in a new world? Would he be someone familiar to talk to when the new people knew nothing about her?

Not at all. Lucky still sits atop the shelf—covered in enough dust to fill a sandbox I suspect! Meanwhile, Mommy tried to foist Gore, the gorilla, on Mel, shipping him to her a few weeks after she'd headed south. At school, she lifted opened the box. After Gore emerged, she immediately texted me: "You're nuts, but thanx." Next trip home, she returned Gore to the shelf. She didn't need him, nor Lucky—whom I wouldn't even think of shipping to college; it would have been too risky to lose him.

So after all these years, we were lucky to stumble upon Lucky that day long ago. But now I think it's really Mom who retains the fondest memories of him, because he's the link to my little girl's little girl years. Having her has been one of the luckiest things in my life. So maybe it's no coincidence that this particular black and white Dalmatian beckoned to her at Bloomingdales that day, as she held her arms outstretched and said, "Hold, hold, hold."

ꕥ

Dorchester Dreams

By Claudia A. Fox Tree

(From a prompt of a photograph of a dog with shaggy hair floating on a raft.)

My name is Eloise and I spend my days soaking up the sun while I relax, floating on a comfortable chair in my whale-shaped swimming pool filled with clear water which reflects its azure blue walls. Well, actually, my name is really Elena and my pool is the roof of our apartment complex and my chair is an inflatable, plastic water raft. This is where I come to escape the mentality of these projects. I can't move forward when I can only see myself here. I need to go to that place where I can be someone else; the place where I can be Eloise. On the outside, people see a poor girl from the projects with a haircut from her mother, shagging my light brown hair. My best friend Devon dyed a blond, almost white, streak on the right side. He said that it would make me more confident. It's a little "Cruella DeVille," only much straighter. Even my hair doesn't fit into the neighborhood where all the girls have dark brunette or black hair that's wavy, curly, or kinky. They say I have "good" hair, but it's not good enough to feel like I fit in. At least I'm short. I can hide in a crowd, should I be so lucky as to be in one. I love to read and can lounge in my "pool" for hours, away from the questioning glares of friends who wonder what makes me too good to hang with them and why I care so much about reading and school. That's another issue.

The phone rang in the classroom yesterday and Ms. Magee whispered a few short words into the receiver: "Ms. Magee's room," "Yes," "Ah huh," "I see," and "Okay, I'll do that." Thirty pairs of eyes watched her place the phone back on its carriage, scan the room, and walk, oh my God, right over to me. "Elena, please take your belongings and walk to the office."

"Elena's going to the principal's office."

"Oooooo, Elena's in trouble," a few voices mumbled under their breath, so that Ms. Magee could barely hear them, but I could. And I didn't know what was going on.

Ms. Winston was a tall, sophisticated woman who always wore pantyhose, even on hot days, and high heels under a smart, dark suit. As I was ushered into her office, I noticed that she was holding a piece of paper in her left hand as she sat behind her small oak desk. "Elena, I have some good news for you."

ꙮ

Give Only to Those Who Say Thank You

By Bruce Nickerson

"Paolo, got a minute?" I asked.

"Sure." We walked into the office and shut the door.

"That your girlfriend? In the car you were driving?"

"Yeah, nice, huh?" he responded with a silly grin on his handsome face.

"She married?"

Looking me straight in the face with a smirk "Yeah. But not to me."

"She know you're HIV positive?" I ask.

"Nah."

"You two fucking?"

"The pope Catholic?" he said exasperatedly.

"You using rubbers?"

"C'mon man. We don't like them. You know what I mean."

"Paolo, you're HIV positive, she has two kids."

"Yeah, but last blood test my T cell count way down. So I'm safe." Off he walked.

Paulo was the youngest in a residence for adults living with HIV and AIDs run by a religious charity, and I was recently hired staff. The charity's operations were behind schedule and under review by funding agencies. I was to update agency-required, behaviorally-oriented treatment plans for house residents. "Other duties as assigned" included giving medications to Paolo and other house residents. And loading the cassettes in which each resident's meds were stored. A bit apprehensive, I asked the slovenly, fat and overweight house manager, "Don't I have to be certified for disbursing meds and loading the cassettes?"

"Well, actually, yes, and anyway, the Visiting Nurse checks them." She replied with an uncomfortable look on her face.

"Oh, you're certified then, and I do this under your supervision?"

"I used to be certified when I worked as an RN, but we don't need it here," she smiled.

"So, I load the cassettes, the Visiting Nurse checks them, and it's ok?" I asked, puzzled.

"Yeah, if she checks them just before the residents get them. But if she doesn't get a chance, I guess it's ok. We've never had a problem."

"OK," I said uncertainly. "We have a written policy on this?"

"Not really, but everyone knows what's going on. And besides, we don't *dispense* drugs, we give the cassette to the resident and the resident takes them."

Later that day I was at the charity's main building and saw a long line of people stretching nervously down the sidewalk and around the corner, like a sidewinder snake wriggling across the sand. Women of all ages, some with kids in tow, and an occasional man looking down on his luck. I asked one of them what the line was all about.

"Weekly groceries."

There was a truck in the driveway, a chute leading to the cellar and some people unloading cartons. "Can I help?" I asked.

"Sure, why don't you go down the cellar and help stack stuff?"

So I went and saw the food pantry manager stacking cartons from the regional food bank. Pleased with this show of egalitarianism, I pitched in. During a break, I said to him "Well, this sure is where the gospel hits the road. Don't know how many people you feed, but that line outside is long."

"Not sure how many we serve 'cuz I'm behind in my paperwork. But it's in the hundreds each week," he responded smugly. He continued, with a look of disgust on his face, "and some of those people don't really need the stuff. They take it cuz it's free. And don't even say 'thank you.'"

"Do you give groceries only to those who say 'thank you,' or give to everyone until the groceries give out?" I asked.

He shot me a puzzled (angry?) look. "Well, if we could, only to those who say 'thank you.' Those who really appreciate it. What do you think?"

"Well, last Sunday's gospel was about Jesus healing ten lepers, and only one came back to thank him, but all ten were healed," I said. I have a big mouth.

Continuing to work, he said, "Well, there's a lot left to stack, we better get at it."

A few weeks later the Director of the charity asked to see me in her office.

I entered the paneled and well-appointed office. The well-dressed director, with carefully coiffed hair, got up from behind her desk, which was flanked by an American flag and two slightly less-than-life-sized religious statues, Joseph on one side, Mary on the other. She closed the door. Not a good sign. There was a look of concern on her face. She walked back and sat down behind her desk as I remained standing awkwardly facing the director and two-thirds of the holy family. I heard the agency had passed its reviews with flying colors, the food bank reports were up to date, and my treatment plans had been complimented. I wondered what our meeting was about.

"I'm afraid I have some bad news," she began. "We've had some budget cuts and will have to let you go."

"I'm sorry to hear that," I responded.

"Well, actually, there were a few other things."

"Oh?"

"We're also worried about the way you dispense drugs to residents. We were afraid that you were not handling them properly and might make mistakes."

"And what else?" I queried, trying to stay calm.

"There is also talk that you don't approve of our food pantry policies."

"I see. Then perhaps I'd better leave now, rather than try to finish the day."

"We are sorry to see you go and wish our budget had allowed us to keep you on." Her voice rang hollow in my ears.

"Thank you. Goodbye." I turned, opened the door, left the office, got in my car, and drove home, leaving her and the statuary behind the desk.

ꕥ

Adirondack Chairs

By Bob Beckwith

Did the original photographer really know just how profound this simple little picture can be? Prints of this work, as well as many variations of it, are sold in gift shops all along the east coast. Such is the case in Perkins Cove in Ogunquit, Maine, where my wife, Carolyn, and I spend several days each year. Maine is a very special place for both of us. We met in Acadia National Park in northern Maine at age eleven, were engaged in the park nine years later and spent a nine-week honeymoon there.

Perkins Cove is where Carolyn and I go to reminisce about old times and to seek renewal. It's mainly a walking area—where one can view the massive rocks and coastline, enjoy the smell of the fresh salt air and watch the sea roll in and out. It's a place where one can unwind, relax, forget your cares and reflect. Some of my best thinking has occurred on jaunts to this cherished spot. One of my most profound thoughts occurred after viewing the Adirondack Chairs' print--one more time.

Upon first seeing this picture, I probably had the same thoughts as many others—what a pretty little picture—such calming colors, a serene setting—just what summer on the ocean should look like. I'll bet many people purchase this picture mainly for these reasons or perhaps as a remembrance of a lovely vacation. The two chairs might remind some of new friendships made or perhaps sharing time together with that very special someone.

During one of our trips to Maine I was apparently in a melancholy mood. Upon seeing this picture, I looked at the empty chairs and began thinking of some of the important people in my life who have passed on—my father-in-law who died when Carolyn and I were just twenty-two years old, my mother who died when we were in our thirties. I thought, "Oh if I could just sit down with them again and listen to more of their wonderful wisdom." My mind wandered even more as I thought how my mother instilled in me, ever since I was a little boy, that I did not have any major disabilities, at least none that should hold me back. She would say, with such a loving smile, "Don't let anyone tell you you can't do something—if you want it badly enough, you'll find a way." I looked away from the picture to kind of pull myself together and I said in my mind, "Oh, to have her sit down with me in these chairs and say those words to me just one more time."

When I glanced back at the picture, a thought—no a command—raced through my head. It said, "Bob, stop concentrating on the chairs—raise your eyes, Bob, what do you see?"

"The ocean," I replied.

"Very good—now think about this, think about this."

That day we did our usual things in the Cove—we walked the rolling, winding three quarter-mile footpath high above the ocean called the Marginal Way. As always, we enjoyed viewing the foaming sea as it slapped high onto the rocks. We watched lobster boats slice through the whipped cream-dolloped blue water following their buoy roadmaps. And finally we browsed through our favorite gift shops. After that, we ate at the outdoor patio restaurant overlooking the tranquil harbor. However, all through our meal my mind kept returning to those words, "Raise your eyes—raise your eyes—just think about this."

Suddenly a wave of calmness swept over me in a way I had never before experienced. Looking out over the harbor, it hit me—my mother is always sitting in that Adirondack chair—right next to me. What I long to have her tell me has not died. No, I simply have to look up and out and view the big picture. She taught me well, to have faith in God and to believe in myself. It is up to me to remember well—and continue to believe well, just as I did when she was alive.

Now whenever I come upon this picture, I break into a relaxed smile. For in those chairs I see the people who have helped make me who I am today—my father-in-law who taught me common sense and street smarts, my mother who would not let me dwell on what I lacked, and my wife, who to this very day encourages me to take chances I would never dream of doing on my own.

Adirondack Chairs—the simple little picture that taught me how to raise my eyes to "see" and appreciate the bigger pictures in life.

ꕤ

The Soup Kitchen

By Bruce Nickerson

I walked into the small, overheated stuffy office for our weekly staff meeting. Andrea, the rector, was there, her gangly body looking uncomfortable on the wooden office chair, her pinched sour face more unpleasant than usual and her short mousy hair typically unkempt. The light from the window behind her dazzled my eyes, making it hard to look her in the face. On her left sat Frank, the assistant rector, with his cherubic, round smiling face looking comfortable as usual, and on his right, behind a computer screen, sat the awkwardly pregnant parish administrator Nicole. I had been hired to manage the parish soup kitchen ministry to the homeless.

"Let's get right to the important issues today," Andrea began suddenly. "Bruce, you've got to tell Fred he can't be in this building unless you're here." Fred was one of our regular homeless clients who also volunteered in the soup kitchen.

"Is there a problem?" I asked.

Not being aware of any observed or reported untoward behavior by Fred, I told Andrea that I was present at the soup kitchen only weekdays. "Well then you have to tell him he cannot be here at coffee hour." Sunday coffee hour after the service is sometimes called the Episcopalians' eighth sacrament.

"What's the problem?"

"He scares people."

"And how does he do that?" I asked curiously.

"He sits in the middle of the floor in that chair of yours and dozes off, and people get scared."

"You mean he sits there, does nothing, dozes and that scares people?"

"Yes it does" she said huffily. "People know he is an addict."

"Does he do anything other than doze off?"

"No."

"And people are scared of that?" I asked, hoping my voice was clear of the anger I was feeling about yet another of her criticisms of the soup kitchen and its homeless clients.

"Yes, and I want you to tell him he cannot be here unless you are here too." She fidgeted in her chair nervously, skinny claw-like hands clasping and unclasping in her lap as if they weren't quite sure where they belonged.

I had a mental image of Fred in his favorite wobbly, rolling office chair, sitting in his usual place in the corner I used for an office. I pictured him dozing and occasionally twitching upright as the chair tilted precariously while upper middle class parishioners politely sipped coffee and carefully nibbled their cake so as not to spill crumbs on the floor. I imagined them chatting about mostly nothing in a brightly lit parish hall whose walls were lined with locked cabinets storing canned food we would make into lunches and suppers for the homeless, one of whom was being blissfully ignored by the very people who were supposed to minister to him.

"Well, people know he's an addict," Andrea continued huffily. Fred didn't hide his addiction from staff. He told me once he was on the methadone program, but I suspected he also supplemented between clinic appointments.

With more sarcasm than intended, I responded, "Perhaps we need to talk about how we tell addicts and other hurting people they are not welcome in this church." The meeting somehow played itself out with no further verbal swordplay.

Andrea was right to suspect Fred of being less than pure. Although, unlike many of his homeless peers, he kept himself neatly dressed and groomed, he was after all an addict, and like all of us addicts, not to be trusted.

We had just received a donation of warm socks, much sought after by our clients for the impending winter, and stored them out of sight in the dark recesses of the church's cellar behind a seldom locked door. Another regular told me that he had "Just seen Fred down the farmers' market selling them socks." I checked the pile of stored socks. It had decreased markedly.

"Fred, can we talk?"

"Yeah, 'sup?"

"In my office." We sat down. I didn't like this. I dislike confrontation and Fred was one of my favorite people. I said, "People say they've seen you at the market selling socks. I'll say this only once. You're an addict. Addicts and alcoholics lie. I know because I'm an alcoholic. We lie very well. I'll take any answer you give me, but if I ever find you stealing from here, your ass is grass, and you're outta here. Understood?"

Sitting straight up and looking me straight in the eyes he said, "Yeah. I did *not* steal those socks."

Every day after that, Fred insisted I search his backpack before leaving. I told him that was not necessary because I had accepted his answer. He insisted. So I did. Reluctantly. Problem solved. No more socks went missing.

Issue not closed. About a week later, Andrea stormed across the parish hall, echoing in its middle-of-the-day emptiness. Standing rigidly in front of me, she confronted me about the sock situation, repeating the "word from the street." I told her Fred and I had talked and there were no more socks missing. "Well, I want him out of here," she said angrily.

"Why?" I asked, annoyed at her attitude.

"Well, he scares people. I already told you that," she said impatiently. I looked at her. She started to tremble and screamed in my face. "Well, he's an addict and a thief and I want him out of here."

"I'm not sure it's my job to tell people who can be here and who can't."

"I'm the rector and I'm telling you what to do."

"I can't do that just because of an *allegation* without any actual proof." I didn't remind her that Jesus hung around with people of questionable business ethics (Matthew), women of reputed easy virtue, and the whole band of them was accused of drinking too much (heroin was not much available in the Galilee).

"*I'll* speak to him," she screeched at me as she stomped off across the parish hall, heels again echoing in the empty space.

As I left that day, Fred was sitting on the steps of the church, bent over with forearms on his knees, hands clasped, and head hung low. He looked up at me as I got close to him. "Well, that's it, huh?" he asked dispiritedly.

"I guess so." God, I was hurting.

"People don't like us because we live on the street and are addicts."

"You think that about me, Fred?" Did I plead for his answer?

"No."

I didn't see Fred again.

Sometime the next summer there was a short item on the third or fourth page of the paper that an "adult male" was found on the Common, not far from the church, dead from an apparent overdose. Heroin. "Word from the street" told me it was Fred.

ഌ☙

Barnes & Noble

By Linda Christen

As a rule I don't like the big megastores, their cavernous interiors with bright lights glaring into your eyes, racks and shelves containing an overwhelming array of choices. Are choices always such a good thing? Can't they be numbing? Despite the size and brightness, or possibly due to them, the megastores feel impersonal; this alienation the embodiment of becoming just another number among the throngs permeates ones sense of self.

This Barnes & Noble is different though, somehow they have managed to create a place devoid of the overwhelming sense of one's ultimate unimportance to the world. In here you're not aware of the underlying need, or rather, corporate desire for profit. This place is comfortable. Carpets, soft lighting, tables and chairs nestled among the stacks of books and in secluded corners. Like a street café, a Starbucks is off to the side where you can sit in the window at a little bistro table, or face the shoppers.

Many predict that the book will go by the wayside, like the candle snuffer and horse-drawn carriage—a relic, possibly surviving only among the overly sentimental or romantic, but in truth no longer necessary. How sad to descend to numbers no longer even recognized, like the nineteenth wife, replaced, or the sad fate of the aged in an ageist society.

This place defies prediction. The "contemporary street café"—relics preserved not for the oddly sentimental but for the human condition; to be among people, possibly anonymous in company but not merely a number. Barnes and Noble serves as a meeting place, a purchase-only library, local café and gift shop. Cavernous, potentially alienating construction turned village.

Today's characters include a DJ meeting with the groom, his bride and her mother. They are going over the ceremony, which traditions and songs to keep, which to discard and what new traditions or songs to add. Possibly mirroring an earlier corporate discussion packed with studies and statistics to design this very meeting place!

A young woman sits facing the window, ear pods in, studying from an oversized text. People are on their phones, or reading books they brought and some from the shelves. They stay here, slow down, hang out and then they eat, sip coffee and browse. While browsing they find things to buy.

Life is spent here, families amble through, lumbering parents striving to keep pace with their eager progeny. Old friends visit and singles meet prospective dates. Some people buy academic texts or classic and contemporary fiction. The new is not only sleek, polished and isolating, here community is the old, archaic and traditional melded with the contemporary.

The book is not obsolete, or only surviving for sentiment; the book and the bookstore are evolving with the postmodern world; providing a new, yet familiar village.

ꙮ

Observing Cybele

By Claudia A. Fox Tree

Her left hand shakes as she reaches into her glossy handbag covered with black and white images from the movie Casablanca. Cybele's blond ponytail is askew to one side of her pale freckled skin and her pink extra-large tunic with white leaf and flower designs hangs asymmetrically off her right shoulder. Her ample size is evident, and no bra or tank-top strap is visible where her skin is exposed in the air-conditioned café. Her calves poke out from her clam-digger pants.

Cybele is in her late thirties and sits by herself at a small wooden table. Her raspberry lemonade forms a puddle as the ice condenses on the side of the plastic container. After a few seconds, Henry joins her. For the previous thirty minutes, Henry has been engrossed in a newspaper on a green velvet sofa a few feet away. Cybele produces two dollars from inside her purse and passes them over to Henry. Her eyes never lift, as though blind, with nothing on which she needs to focus.

How was your day?" he asks.

"Fine." Then there is silence.

"That's a pretty color on you. Did you tie your hair up by yourself today?"

"Dotty did it," she says, still staring down to her right. Henry reaches over the space between them and pushes a stray piece of her left bang back behind her ear. Then his seventy-something hand disappears in front of him into a paper bag that rips a little, like the hole in his heart. He pulls out a muffin and begins to cut it into small finger-holding-sized pieces and places them on a napkin in front of Cybele.

ꕥ

Eating Alone

By Katherine Picard

Eating is a necessary evil and sometimes we find ourselves having to eat alone. That's not necessarily a bad thing. You can go to the restaurant of your choice, browse the menu, order what you want and enjoy your food at your pace. If you are in a foreign country, you get experience in maneuvering around the menu, as well as ordering in a foreign language. Hopefully, when the food arrives, it is what you had wanted to order. Finally, you get to handle the country's "funny money" when the bill comes.

Sometimes, you get to meet some interesting locals or at the very least you can be a voyeur without sneaking around. The best part of dining alone is watching the other diners, wherever you may be.

Perhaps being an only child, as well as a frequent "accompanying person" on my husband's foreign business trips, has prepared me more thoroughly than some who find it necessary to dine alone.

On one occasion, my husband and I were having supper at the intimate Japanese restaurant in Bedford Center. Seated to our left was an older couple who spent their time, before their meals came, reading books. When their food was graciously presented, they accessed it, started to eat and each, as on cue, picked up their book and continued reading. No conversation ensued over dinner. In essence they were eating alone—together.

ꕥ

Little Freddie

By Bruce Nickerson

Note: Little Freddie's vocabulary is neither pretty not politically correct, but Bruce uses his language to help you understand Little Freddie better.

"Fuck you asshole! What, you 'fraid to get outta that shitcan cab you're driving?"

You could hear Little Freddie shouting over the bumper-to-bumper traffic of rush hour on the main street not far from the soup kitchen. He could barely stand upright as he staggered between the cars, arms flailing at the air, curses and invective thrown who knows where: at the cab drivers, cars, cabs, trucks, the other pedestrians, at the drizzle covering everything.

"You goddam fucking nigger. You come over here, can't even speak the language, and you shitheads take all our jobs." His drunken tirade was slurred almost beyond understanding.

When he was sober for a stretch, Little Freddie was a sweet guy. His nickname distinguished him from Freddie, a slightly bigger soup kitchen regular. Little Freddie was five-foot-six or shorter, slightly built, with short cropped dark hair and an engaging, almost elfin, face. He would help in the kitchen, and with other chores, rushing quietly and efficiently around the area. He had the gift of "helps" as St Paul would call it. He was at the right place at the right time and didn't need to be told what to do—he was already there washing dishes, clearing tables, sweeping up, and so on.

In those sober periods, Little Freddie would move back into his girlfriend's apartment. Brenda had gotten her act together; been sober a few years now, had a responsible paraprofessional job in a good company, and was a success story.

When Little Freddie went on a "run," Brenda would gather up his belongings, throw them into the street, and change the locks on her doors. During his runs, the dark side of his personality emerged. The received wisdom at the kitchen was that addicts were easier to host than alcoholics. Addicts would sit there nodding, and the most trouble they caused was a staff member having to hoist their faces out of their soup or mashed potatoes after they had slumped into their menu for the evening, or waking them to escort them to their beds whose location they had forgotten. Alcoholics, however, would frequently get mean and belligerent. And so it was with Little Freddie.

When he was on a run, we would ban Little Freddie from the soup kitchen. Then he would take to the sidewalks and streets, picking, and losing, fights with anyone or anything that moved including pedestrians or cars in rush hour traffic. It was rumored he sometimes picked fights with people who weren't there at all. He lost these too.

Little Freddie had been through a number of "detoxes." Not sure how many. Some people endure fifty or more detoxes. We called the short ones "spin dries." Occasionally Little Freddie would get maudlin and weepy, crying that he needed to get to a detox and "this time really get my act together." Conned again, the staff would chip in, call a taxi, stuff Little Freddie inside it, and tip the driver to get him to the nearest detox with a bed—and to be careful not to let him get out until he got to the detox. Just as frequently, Little Freddie managed to hop out of the cab and start in again.

One dark, cold and sleeting morning, on the way to the soup kitchen, when my mood matched the weather, I met Brenda. She was walking to work. Happened often enough that I looked forward to the chance encounters.

"How's Freddie?"

"Gone again."

"Aw shit. When?" I asked.

"Last Saturday. Picked a fight with a cab."

"Cabbie beat him up?"

"Not the cabbie, the CAB!" A disappointed smile, seemingly at the hopelessness of the situation. Or perhaps the absurdity of Freddie fighting with an automobile.

"So you threw his stuff out?"

"Yeah."

"When you gonna get rid of him?

"Dunno. We have a long history together and he grows on you."

"I know. Especially when he's sober."

"Yeah," she said, with a soft winning smile.

My melancholy kicked into overdrive. "Dammit, Brenda, I thought I was going to save the world through this soup kitchen." I paused. "Then when something like Freddie comes up, I realize all we're doing is giving out a sandwich and a cup of soup."

She stopped walking. She turned in her attractive long coat buttoned against the wind and rain, umbrella protecting her carefully coiffed hair. She looked me in the face wistfully, and said, "You know, Freddie and I lived on the streets together for a few years. In shelters. Under bridges. Alleys. Sometimes went dumpster-diving for food or the leftovers from someone's bottle. Summer, winter."

"Yeah I know."

"And until you've done that, you will never know how good that soup and sandwich tastes on a cold nasty day like what we get there. Don't you ever forget that."

We were at her street crossing. She waited for the traffic light, then crossed the street busy with the morning rush hour traffic. I turned right to the soup kitchen.

Postscript: Last Wednesday afternoon I heard that Brenda was now director of the soup kitchen and that Little Freddie had died a few years ago. I do not yet have any more details.

ᘛᘚ

333 North 11th Street…

By Katherine Picard

Mentally it's the 1940s. I walk down the back alley from our house on Lehman Street, turn left at 11th Street, and walk the block or so to my grandparents' house. It's a short walk, straight down 11th. Weidman Street runs into 11th, perpendicularly, halfway down. I keep walking straight, not becoming distracted by the appearance of the other street, until I come to the two-way intersection. Carefully manipulating the intersection, I cross over to their side of the street. A few houses down is their house. Shingled, number 333; part of the row houses that make up the neighborhood in Lebanon, Pennsylvania.

Stairs run up to the front door, but they are rarely used. Instead, I walk the narrow, dark tunnel-like path between the conjoined houses until I reach two doors at the end. The neighbor's door is on the right, Mom and Pop's on the left. This path always felt dark and creepy, like someone could be waiting at the end where the two doors met. It was especially scary if you had just seen an *Abbott and Costello* meets *Frankenstein* movie! I was sure there would be someone there in wait as I went ever so slowly down the connecting tunnel.

Walking through the door at the end, light appears and you enter the outer porch with its Hoosier for storage and the wringer washing machine on one side; the door to the kitchen is on the left, and straight ahead is the door to the back yard. If you went out to the backyard there was my Uncle Henry's pigeon coop, Pop's garden and rose bushes and further down along the walk you found the chicken coop. At the end is the gate that will take you to the back alley that ran behind the entire row of houses.

But my trip has gotten sidetracked. I enter the door leading to the kitchen—it's small with a cook stove and coal bucket, and a sink along the wall ahead of you, a table and chairs on the left, and on the right is a staircase leading up to the bedrooms. Under the staircase is storage with a door to access whatever treasures were under those stairs. My grandmother always sat in a straight-back chair in front of that door with her ever-present crochet hook in her hands with beautiful edging coming off the end of the hook.

If you went left by the edge of the table, you entered the dining room—with a TV—where I watched Dick Clark after school before his *Bandstand* show from Philly became famous. Going through the dining room was the more formal front room across from which were the other set of stairs that took you up stairs. Nobody ever used the front room, and I can't remember ever eating in the dining room; we always sat in the kitchen.

Either the front or back stairs would take you upstairs to the bedrooms, bath, and the sun porch, which was above the porch downstairs. I don't remember much about those rooms except my Grandpop had a black Big Ben alarm clock in their bedroom at the top of the stairs. There was an open area with closets and drawers for clothing.

My Grandpop would allow me to help him in his garden. My job was to capture the Japanese beetles off his roses into a jar of kerosene. I was delighted to do this with him! Sometimes we went into the chicken coop, but I wasn't keen on doing that as one day a rooster jumped on my back when I was bending down.

My maternal grandparents, Wendel and Katherine Kundus Risko, were from Czechoslovakia, but they were Slovak and not Czech! According to my grandfather, the Czechs were gypsies. The neighboring streets housed many other Slovak families and a few blocks away were the Slovak church and school named after Saints Cyril and Methodius! I went to this church and school as did my aunts and uncles before me.

One time in the 1960s, my grandfather came to Massachusetts and visited my parents and me in our house in West Newton. In Slovak, Grandpop asked my mom, his daughter Mary, how much our house cost. She told him $21,000. He asked her why she bought such an expensive house, explaining that his house on 11th street only cost him $1000! My mom smiled and explained to him that her taxes were more than that!

My Aunt Rosie still lives in that house. She's 79 now and raised six children there. My Uncle Henry lived with her, too, in his later years after having spent his life in the U.S. Navy. My grandparents had raised twelve children in that house and later a grandson, too. He was slightly younger than me—I being the oldest grandchild and also named after my grandmother.

The ethnicity of the neighborhood has changed. One bishop even changed the name of the church. My Aunt Caroline was furious and wrote him a letter telling him that his action was most disrespectful to the Slovak people who had built that church.

I haven't seen this house for many years. I keep wanting to but somehow never do… Maybe soon…

10

NATURE

We sometimes use nature as our prompt, creating nature metaphors to try to understand life's problems and concerns. Here are examples.

How Can I Help My Children Stop Fighting?

By Jennifer Klein

The ground here is covered with mulch. Mulch to prevent the weeds from sprouting and to keep the soil moist. It sounds hollow when you pound it. Like a drum. It was a strange surprise to me to hear that noise. I wonder if Corinna felt a similar sense of surprise when she first realized she could make her older sister cry.

This morning Rachel and Corinna were trying on their school clothes. Rachel's were new. Corinna's were hand-me-downs.

"Mine had better come in bags," Corinna told me as I went to retrieve hers from my bedroom closet. In packaging from the company, she meant.

They didn't, but she liked them anyway. She and Rachel admired themselves in the mirror.

"You don't look beautiful," Corinna told Rachel.

She was like me—pounding the earth to discover the noise that it made.

Rachel let out a whine, or some sort of pathetic noise, in response.

Parenting books say even younger sisters don't like to share their parents. Here the forest ground cover, the clover, and the baby maple trees, show their green faces toward the sun. Each is trying to reach higher than the other to get the full attention of the sun's warmth. Just like my Corinna. She wants to grow taller, and she wants to soak up as much of Rachel's sunlight as she can. Still, the clover and the three-leafed plants grow, even while all those other plants compete with them.

There is a chilly wind out today. The ants are scurrying along, climbing short sticks, which to them must seem so high off the ground. They are searching for their food. One tiny ant is now on my sandal, but it has decided it doesn't like the texture; now it is back on the exposed root that has grown its way from the woods, across the grassy, mossy patch, and onto the mulch. A pair of ants is leap-frogging its way over to the mulchy part. Perhaps they are foraging for some pine sap. I see several trails of the sap on the black rubber tubing that was accidentally left around the base of this tree.

Deeper in the woods, the ground-cover plants cannot grow. The tall maples and pines block their light. But smaller trees flourish. They have enough distance between them to grow happily, and they catch the scattered rays of the sunny patches that make it through as the trees sway in the breeze. Or maybe they just sway because it is so difficult to stand very still for a very long time—even if you are a tree, with your massive root system anchoring your one long leg—or maybe it's one long body. Trees are kind of like up-side-down people. We have one main body, and two legs, while they have one body, sticking into the ground with all of these limbs coming every which way out the top. More, the higher you go. Their massive heads are stuck in the ground with hundreds of tongues searching under the ground for water.

So we've decided to give the girls some alone time with each parent every weekend. Some time so that they can find their own sunlight, before they come back home and stick their heads in the ground, kicking each other around our dinner table. Or maybe they are just moving around to let the sunny patches through.

ꕤ

The Alabaster Vase

By Charlotte Christen

I

An Egyptian alabaster vase sits in the center of the elongated teak table extended for a family dinner, a space for everybody. We are a small group. We all fit comfortably around the table. The family isn't growing larger as one pictures descendants on a genealogy chart fanning out from an immigrant couple. Forty-seven years and a two-board table can still seat the entire family, with space even for unrelated guests.

The vase, with its veins of rust and deep brown swirls, reminds me of the large chunks of Halvah we used to buy at the Ann Arbor Farmers' Market back in Michigan when we were a family of four. The flowers in the vase are autumn mums and pale yellow daisies. The bronze and gold mums and the daisies are set off by several short stalks of lemon leaves. All are cut down in size from the way they were last week on Thanksgiving Day. Then, they filled a much larger crystal vase that included stalks of fragile pink and purple blossoms, blossoms that were quick to fade, droop and die, blossoms removed and discarded when the bouquet was trimmed down to fit the smaller alabaster vase. It is still a bouquet, still pleasing to look at, just as precious as the original Thanksgiving centerpiece, only smaller.

In a day or two, this arrangement in the alabaster vase will also be cut down. Next to droop and die will be the pale yellow daisies. Already their heads are bending toward the tabletop. The remaining flowers will then be placed in a still smaller vase and the procedure will be repeated a few more times, always removing and discarding the dead floral stems until perhaps my miniature Mexican pottery vase containing a single sturdy miniature bronze mum will be displayed in the center of the table.

II

The sky is beginning to lighten; the trees outside the windows on the side door are still green, still alive despite it being well into the autumn months. It is December—they must be evergreens. Later I will open the door to look more closely, but logically I know there are no green deciduous trees still retaining their leaves in December.

In front of me, alongside my cup of coffee, is the alabaster vase with the remaining flowers from the Thanksgiving centerpiece getting older and droopier, yet still able to present an appearance of being a viable flower arrangement. If it wasn't known they were trimmed down from a much larger and more luxurious bouquet, it might not be evident, but I know, so therefore to me it is a diminished centerpiece on a too-long teak dining table where the small troupe of family and near-family members sat to eat, talk and play cards just one week ago.

The curtains are still closed over the windows and slider door; only the light of the rising sun is visible there, starting to shine through the gold color of the translucent linen curtains. It is a perfect backdrop for the vase of gold and bronze blossoms highlighted by the green of the lemon leaves and the green glow from the windows on the door. Harmonious. Sparse, yet harmonious.

Looking closely, I see it won't be necessary to cut back the stems today. No need to find a smaller vase for shortened flowers; no need to discard dead blossoms.

III

The overhead kitchen light shines on the alabaster vase causing it to glow like a hard wax sculpture or a lightly polished granite urn, not like the chunk of Halvah it brought to mind earlier. Today it reminds me of a Van Gogh painting. Perhaps I will sketch it. I could have done that with the full centerpiece a week ago, then continued to sketch it at vase-changing intervals—a pictorial biography of a Thanksgiving centerpiece illustrating the beauty in the progression from its zenith to its demise, recorded and preserved for the future, like the photographs in the albums lined up on my bookshelves.

No green is visible outside the windows, no sunshine. The curtains are drawn shut and with only darkness outdoors their translucency isn't apparent. Now another room exists beyond the windows on the side door, a reflection of the room I am in. If I lean to the right I am able to acknowledge another person dressed like me, also sitting at a table.

The flowers in the Egyptian alabaster vase suffered a bit since I last examined them. The lower petals on the golden mums are turning downward, the heads on some of the yellow daisies seem too heavy for their stems; they are beginning to bend alarmingly about a thumbs breadth down from the blossoms.

There is something new alongside the vase tonight, a handmade book covered with handmade marbled paper. It is a guest book with the signatures and messages of visitors to the house during the past thirty years. Some of the messages are from people gone—just like the discarded flowers from the Thanksgiving centerpiece. Other messages are from family members still a part of the groups that sit around the table for special times. Still others are from friends or relatives who, like the yellow daisies and golden mums, are in precarious situations and may not be in the vase much longer. This latter group of flowers or people needs to be carefully watched.

I envy those family groupings whose reunions and celebrations are so large they need to rent a function hall to hold them. At a recent family wedding, the blood relatives of the groom fit around one small round table with room for a few close friends. Perhaps that is why I watch carefully over the alabaster vase and its diminishing bouquet; each flower is precious, and they become more so as the bouquet dwindles down to smaller and smaller proportions.

ജ്ജ

Snap. Reach. Snap. Snap. Snap.

By Linda Christen

There is something undeniably primeval and satisfying to the deepest recesses of the soul, tending flowers. This time of year it is the Lilies. As a child it was Petunias, their wilted petals leaving a sweet sticky sap on my fingers. As they die, their heads dip toward the ground, the scent strengthens, color fades, their sap seems pushed to the surface. Lilies don't weep sugar; they shrivel and fade. Turning to face the earth; wrinkled shells of their once-vibrant blossoms.

Dead buds are useful for dying cloth into a subdued orange, more functional in their dull ending than in their vibrant youth! Not so with Petunias; they are merely flashy splashes of hot pink and royal purple, lush through the summer but unable to return another year.

Thus the term "annuals" in reference to their delicate constitution. The Lily, she strengthens and returns every year, thicker, multiplying clusters of life. She resides along the sides of country roads, in "naturalized" clumps, among plainer friends across country fields, organic sunset thrusts filling pockets of urban nature and littering suburban yards.

Picture the crisp "snap." Put your thumb and forefinger on either side of a distinctive curve at the base of each faded bloom, slide your fingers toward each other, and give a decisive twist of your wrist to separate the bloom from its origin. I drop it in the garden where it will decompose, feeding the soil for next year's Lilies.

If I had the time, need, or inclination toward expanses of orange cloth or yarn, I cold boil them for their dye. But this pastoral practicality is no longer efficient. With the speed of rationalized production, globalization, monopoly capitalism, modernism and scientific thought, it is now "smarter" to purchase orange clothing.

The redundant bloom no longer necessary for anything but the nutrients it releases in decomposition. Some people don't even reap this. They throw the unsightly dead flesh away, preferring to purchase a bottle of sterile chemical fertilizing concoction—a liquid, powder or stick to feed next year's growth.

All of this, every iota of feeling, thought, memory, history, modernism and future are encompassed in that one quick, satisfying "snap." How can this seemingly insignificant action carry so much?

Walking along a city garden, country road or my own yard, I find it meditative to work my way through an entire flower bed, plucking and snapping, "dead heading." It's a rhythmic, "pop pop pop," at once rebellion and acquiescence.

Despite all the changes our world has seen, these flowers continue. People tend them, reaping whatever benefits the blossom offers and they need.

ജ്ജ

I Sit on My Porch

By Kathleen Shure

I sit on my porch,

Noticing the berry vine

Having worked its way through the lattice

Into the darkness under the porch

In hopes of finding another way up

Between the crevices of the floor boards

To find the warmth and light.

I feel like the vine,

Reaching out, hopeful,

That through all the tangles of life

I will one more time

Find a golden, sun-filled way.

ꕥ

It is What It Is

By Linda Christen

A baby pine tree clung to the edges of the great stone outcropping. It tilted its emerald face toward the vivid light which bounced off the mirror-like surface of the small lake, reflecting a blinding light from the edges of a few cumulous cotton candy clouds drifting on the day's gentle breeze amidst a perfect blue sky. The sky—not a pure turquoise or cornflower, but somewhere between, close to the blue of soft, well-loved gingham, but not fully any of these. With hope, the baby pine sends its roots into a patch of moss, adhered like cream cheese frosting along the rock, gathering, pooling in the rock's dips and crevasses.

So many greens, those shining like emeralds from fluffs of needles stemming out of four diminutive but promising branches to the moss, a deep green approaching olive, due to the bits of brown stamens among soft carpet, a final shade of green is on the ledge, clusters of lichen scattered in the areas where neither moss nor pine have any hope of survival. Its light oxidized copper flecks stretching out from the center create clusters of circles, like coins nonchalantly dropped on top of the bureau, the random scattering of lichen pennies creates a pattern which somehow makes sense.

The lichen and moss are meant for this challenging landscape. But the little pine will struggle. Being young and optimistic, its little roots can still take hold in the moss and remain deep enough to hold up and balance its trunk and four eager branches with their happy emerald puffs. He can stretch toward the lake, his face to the sun. Indeed at this tender age, our baby pine has what it needs to survive.

Unfortunately, future survival on this rock will not be possible; it cannot support the needs of a young pine tree. The baby pine knows nothing but to put its energy into growing, hoping to someday match the height and strength of the other pines in the wood. It does not yet know that to flourish in this location is not possible; indeed its very survival for another year is questionable.

The baby pine doesn't know the external limits under which he has landed. He doesn't know that due to circumstances beyond control, no matter how beautiful the area might be, our baby pine cannot ever reach his full potential. Our naïve baby pine emits an aura of striving, sunny optimistic joy for life.

But for the hiker passing by, our story would end in futility....

The hiker keeps a steady, slow pace appearing determined and in awe of the fresh spring air. She notes radiant light splashes glistening off the water, plops and rustles as critters of both land and lake scurry away before her. Visibly energized, her eyes glisten with the excited anticipation that only spring can inspire. The greening of the land beginning to reveal signs of the full potential of its summer beauty distracts the hiker from her focus to walk and breath consciously in the fresh air. She obviously enjoys what must be her first hike of the season.

Rounding the curve made by the outcropping of ledge, entranced, is she thinking of picnics with her love, sheltered beneath the shallow cave-like overhang, soft ground beneath and glistening water before them? The overhang is a fascinating, organically created structure. Good for climbing to achieve a new angle from which to observe the lake. Our hiker climbs the outcropping.

She spots our little pine, reminiscent of "The Little Engine that Could," with its will and spirit. Yet so unlike the little engine in the reality of its situation, with no thought of the rules of the environment, "leave nothing but your footsteps and take nothing but your memories," she swoops down and uproots our baby pine.

Perhaps something about its demeanor compelled her to save him. Did she know that to save the little pine meant to find a new location? Yes, away from his woods' worth of mothers, aunts and grandmothers, brought to a new place, where the ancient pine no longer seeds babies for the continuation of the wood. A place in need of baby trees, which offers a wide open sky filled with sunshine. This is a place of soft earth with water flowing just below the surface, where roots can sink as deep as is needed and devote all of one's will solely toward reaching one's fullest potential.

By leaving a home too harsh for survival, our baby pine can reforest a place in need; rejuvenating an ancient wood.

What is right, what is wrong, was the hiker soft hearted or callous?

ℬ⊃𝒞ℛ

11

POETRY

Note: Some poems have been placed earlier in the book under specific sections because they were written in a "regular" class with Mindy Pollack-Fusi, not in a "special" workshop with Dianalee Velie, like these, below.

Father

By Louise St. Germain

arms open wide
    welcoming beckoning
        He calls to me

Silenced, awed,
    bowed in humility
        I call to Him

ethereal light surrounds,
    engulfing, lifting
        I acknowledge Him

He comes for me.

Life Changes at Eleven

By Louise St. Germain

Noises come from the kitchen
In the middle of the night.
I peek in on my way back from the bathroom.
They shooed me back to bed.
Don't look, go away.
Wide awake in my bed
Something must be wrong
Wanting to know, not wanting to know.

Dawn. I creep down the cold hallway
To the voices once more.
I open the door.
The family is in the kitchen.
John, the oldest says Daddy is dead.
Take these books
Alice in Wonderland and Through the Looking Glass
Go away and read, escape.

No tears, no grief, no reassuring hugs
How strange they did not cry
Nor comfort
When life changed for me at eleven.

ꙮ

Ode to Salvador

By Louise St. Germain

Yuk! A spoonful of sugar helps the medicine go down
So they say!
With a tongue like that and a curled up nose
it will take more than a spoonful.
What in the world was he thinking?
Sarah where are you when I need you?
The supposed genius puts brush to canvas and creates.
Viewing his work I critique quite negatively,
I do not understand.

Attempting to interpret the artist
I gag at the monstrosity
with its conical snail like ear,
eyes void of sight,
corded musculature,
white matter exposed,
thinking inside out,
a flattened specimen of human,
back and spirit broken,
the artist and I – we walk to a different tune.

I put pen to paper and create
you come along and view
Is your critique negative?
Can you understand?
Or do you walk to a different tune?

ജ൫

Journeys

By Louise St. Germain

Journeys start unknown to me
one step leads the way
a hand reaches out
"come with me, we'll start the day"
fear is foremost what to expect
what does life expect of me
bogged down by shoulds'
ruled by the Id
I grasp the hand
take a chance
become free.

One step is all it takes
one kind voice
a firm hand in mine
trust, one leap of faith
reach for the horizon
rainbows of hope
peacefulness
sweetest sunrises
begin to own who I am
today I am free
free to just be.

ꕤ

Looking at a Page of Swahili

By Louise St. Germain

Greek-Swahili-Latin
presents itself to me
eye to eye challenging
the creative form

printed words do not matter
the spirit moves the soul
words melt and blend
fusing as one

welcome welcome
all are welcome
take my hand
we'll share our worlds

language is no barrier
when heart and soul meet
reach out my friend
we will all be free

ᘓᘐ

A Person I Admire (Arnold Schwarzenegger)

By George L. Hand

Of all the famous people to pick for this task,
Why pick him, you all may ask?
I have four reasons that add up to a lot.
This man has excelled. He always gave his best shot.
He was a body builder, and at 20 years of age,
Became Mr. Universe. Among the muscular, this is the gauge.
He excelled in business and made quite a pile,
Surpassing most people's success by a mile.
Arnold became a movie star because of his build.
An interesting fact, he was liked though not skilled.
He mostly played parts like a robotic man,
Where you would expect a flat delivery, as part of the plan.
Finally, he was elected governor back in 2003.
This makes four successful endeavors you'll have to agree.
Most of us may aspire to excel in one role.
Maybe a small fraction will reach their goal.
I know of no other who has succeeded four times.
Thus, the "Governator" is the subject of my rhymes.
How would I like to have some relation to him?
I guess watching a movie being filmed is my whim.
To fulfill this wish it's too late now.
Which is okay since I'm not a gushy fan anyhow.
Arnie is known for two sayings, please take note:
"I'll be back," and, "Hasta la vista, Baby," we can quote.

Afterward…
It's an unfortunate problem for successful men.
They have everything but can't control one yen.
You'd think they would take care and not ruin their life
By hurting their family, especially their wife.
A little extracurricular activity, what has it bought?
Their success, even four times, is all for naught.

ꕥ

The Nude

By George L. Hand

Simple, straight forward, a swim alone.
Should we care? No harm done.
The human body, the highest form of art.
Beauty, male or female.
Young and well put together.
We all should be so lucky.

ꕥ

The Tree

By George L. Hand

The edge of a hurricane went through.
Three friends wanted to earn some cash.
Any opportunity would do.
People will have trees down. They'll need cutting.
We found one that seemed pretty large.
"Can we cut up and remove that tree, Sir?"
For $75, that's $25 apiece.
Did we know what we were doing? No.
We worked all day with axe and saw.
A maple tree is easy if still green.
Then the thought, how do we remove it?
Bill knew a guy, he would loan us his dump truck.
For $10 and a solemn promise, return the truck unharmed.
Loading the wood, more work, but where to take it?
The town dump. It was getting dark, the stump remained.
"When you're done, you get paid."
Two guys replied, "Enough, we quit."
I was determined and dumb.
I'll finish and get the money, which I did.
I learned, "One property of wisdom is knowing
When to stop and walk away."
"I think I can," is not always the best idea.

ꕥ

Remembering Ten

By Charlotte Christen

Pretending to sleep,
I pull the quilt over my head.
Mostly, I am an early riser,
Not today.
Today is Sunday.
Which Sunday?
Mom's Sunday?
Dad's Sunday?
Which church?
To which God do I pray today?
Why must I go?
Who or what is God anyhow?
I wish somebody would tell me.
I slide farther down under the quilt.
I hear Dad's voice calling me to get ready for Mass.
It's Catholic Sunday.
Today I will memorize the intricate designs
in the stained glass windows
and breathe in the heavy scent of incense.

ഗ്ദ

Growing Pains

By Mindy Pollack-Fusi

Five was the new house. Brown. The moving truck out the kitchen window giving hope a friend might move in and loneliness dissipate.

Six was snowfall, taller than the top of my head. No matter. Bundled into jacket and threw snowballs for Pixie.

Seven was autumn leaves. Jacket zipped, $5 in pocket, shouting: "I'm leaving! You'll be sorry!" Only I, the sorry one, turned back home—the only solution to frozen fingers and a cracked heart needing warmth.

Eight was tears. Why did Meredith crawl under our dining room table, the party hats and prizes atop it so orderly. "Relax," Mom said, "It's okay." Meredith back in her seat; my party, for me, Over.

Nine was watching the girls walk home, chased by the boys, and the boys asking me where Judi went, where was Carole, where'd Donna go? Passing me by for giggling girls. Strange game.

Ten was laundry bleach, sneaking downstairs, fragile confidence that the washer spinning my new navy blue pants for Pirates of Penzance (that I'd dirtied outside) would produce clean pants. Nope! White spots everywhere. Mom mad. New navy blue pants purchased—too large, none left in my size, so I, shhhh, wore the spotted ones instead. Mom mad again.

Eleven was goodbye. Fifth grade fun—Spin the Bottle, dancing to the hit parade, studying the American Revolution and crying because we were moving there, to Lexington, and thus farewell to my New York days and growing pains.

ജ൜

Turning Fifty

By Mindy Pollack-Fusi

Turning fifty. What to experience, as though, in case, life is
abbreviated, after.

Animals. The connection to my soul.

Choose Africa, a voice deep inside repeatedly sang with words that
eventually reached my consciousness.

Choose Africa.

I chose, not Hawaii, again, where the first time, thunderbolts struck
not only the atmosphere but also the fiber of our marriage.

I chose, not Paris, because Paris I would not do alone; Paris is love,
romance, glistening red wine in the shadows of dim restaurants, legs
entwined under the table, hearts and loins yearning for
after-the-restaurant.

I chose Africa. Brave I, going off alone, with strangers, to see my
beloved animals in their own homes while I left mine—with its
stepfamily tensions—behind, to turn fifty, alone, with strangers.

Turning fifty. No strangers: New family, dusty backpacks filled with
awe, jambo mornings before our java, friends anew, black-skinned
people far away but just like us, yearning for family, love, connection.

I chose. Lions roared and my camera captured mothers protecting
children, babies groomed by clans, nature dealing with death like we
stir turkey carcasses in pots. My photos shown now to zoo patrons,
sick children, photo fanatics. My journey shared.

Turning fifty. A safari toward my own freedom and creativity.
Stretching to limits untamed.

ﾐ

Wishes for My Children

By Claudia A. Fox Tree

I wish to live long enough
To see you have a child
Who may be meek or may be wild.
I want to see you handle stuff.

Some parenting I could easily do.
Some, I wish I'd better done.
Some, I just wasn't "that kind of one."
Most parenting I invented new.

It may not have been the best,
But it's the best I had to give,
To see you grow and live
To leave my handspun nest.

Courage is a silent strength unsearched,
Fear hidden deep beneath,
To hold my tongue and grit my teeth
Your choices made for better… or for worse.

"A big, fat pig too lazy to bring in bags from the store"
After returning from my job as teacher,
And "second shift" as chauffeur,
Were words that surely tore my heart a little more.

I didn't deserve your humiliating name-calling,
Or degrading put-downs, as a matter of fact,
(Though I know your father modeled all of that)
Sometimes I collapsed to bed in exhausted sprawling.

As dishes overflow in sink, on floor, and bureau
And laundry threatens to eat me alive,
I simply can't keep up with all you five
Without you also helping clean the burrow!

A single mom with many responsibilities
Working hard, so your interests can be explored
Isn't asking too much for a single chore
In exchange for your remaining time to be free.

I hope to live at least 25 more years
To see you with your own 17-year-old
And wish nothing less be told
Then he (or she) reflect all of you, my dear.

ꟗꟗ

Chinese Restaurant

By Claudia A. Fox Tree

I'm a glass half full kinda girl
An optimist, so to speak,
Things will work out
There's no place but up
It only gets better
Good luck is what you make it

That is,
As long as I surround myself
With like-minded thinkers
Because I have known
Pressure to bottle feed from non-nursing mothers;
Depths of depression from sad, unhappy people; and
Hating my job from those who were stuck in a rut.
I choose to be happy.

The Year of the Rabbit tells us that
Good luck is only a hop, skip, and jump away
Hop to it!

ꟗꟗ

A Child's Story

By Claudia A. Fox Tree

Silence.
The years go by
and I don't tell no one.
A Dream? Did I imagine it?
It's real.

Cutting
tiny slivers
on my arm, open enough to
release the pain inside my heart…
for now.

Dying
on the inside.
Thinking of suicide,
but the cat is staring at me
blankly.

Molest
an 8 year old?
Why'd he do it to me?
I think I will pretend to be
sleeping.

Sleeping.
I know it's rape,
as I think back on it
now that I am a teenager.
I know.

Silence.
There, I said it.
I hate being thirteen.
Don't want to talk anymore now.
All done.

ℵ

Westward Migration

By Claudia A. Fox Tree

Clamoring for gold in California's hills,
the forty-niners panned, raked, and shook the land
'til what remained was only loose rocks and fill.

1 in 20 was dealt a richer hand
than what fed him in his previous home
That's better odds than most could stand.

Though Sacagawea could walk the path alone,
Lewis and Clark used her because they knew that she
would know the people who needed to be known

Her "Oregon trail" went as far as the eye could see
"Land for the taking…
A new frontier," said Manifest Destiny

The buffalo herds, once grand and racing
disappeared as the railroad ripped and filed
transcontinental tracks with steady pacing.

10 miles a day and 400 rails per mile
brought telegraph and visitors
through gaping holes blown into mountain sides.

The mountain views, the canyon floor,
and changes in the greenery
could not be stopped with this now open door.

Changes in the scenery
was nothing compared to destruction of lives.
The Supreme Court could not even stop the thievery.

The Trail of Tears moved Native People 4,000 miles
away from whence they came.
Promises of a better life, land, and claim. All lies.

After all that, nothing was ever the same.

Last Night's Hair

By Linda Christen

I look in the mirror
Hair, curls knotted together
Sticking out
Frizzy here
Knotted there
Bangs akimbo.

Hopeless
Tricks of the trade
Wet the bangs
Heat and brush
Tame them into order.

Tidy the disorderly jumble
Knots cleared with a brush
Damp hands
Scrunch

Last night's hair
Ready for a new day.
Am I?

ꟾ

Memory

By Linda Christen

Beneath the apple tree
Resting
Overflowing bushels
Brilliant fruit
Backs brush the rough trunk

Each bite sweeter than the last
Mine
Few large chunks removed
Hers
Diminutive nibbles

Like a chipmunk
Hundreds of bites
Around and around
Lips and cheeks
Apple red.

Gone now
Lean against the trunk
Look up through the leaves
Forget Me Not speckles
Between branches, leaves and apples

A moment
Easily lost among millions
Mother and daughter
In the warmth of sun, fruit and love
Basking

ꙮ

Birds

By Linda Christen

Turkeys outside can be seen
They wake me every April.
Clustering under the Maple
They squawk and preen.

Robins arrive when the soil is no longer hard.
Singing loudly,
Their hardy bodies soundly
Hopping about the yard.

I've yet to see the Goldfinch of summer
Who visits once the sun is high.
These little yellow flecks will fly
From thistle to feeder by the number.

Year round the Cardinal is best,
She is plain while he flashes crimson.
The couple appears winsome
As in my wisteria they nest.

ॐ

You Can Never Ask, "But what about the Animals?"

By Jennifer Klein

Hundreds of elephants could die of thirst across the savannah.
Thousands of polar bears could collapse from starvation in the Arctic.
Ocean waves could crash black and heavy with the carcasses of a million oily birds.

If you ask, "What about the animals?"
They will whisper behind your back, "Granola."

You can never say,
"We share this planet with so many other species."
The woods are full of owls, finches, squirrels
Deer, mice, coyotes, fishers.
They want to "develop" these woods.
We say, "We can't develop these woods.
"So many animals live there."
They say, "Coyotes are dangerous."
"And ticks. You know about ticks."

Bats suffer and die from white-nose syndrome.
The few frogs we have left splash out of the rivers and streams with missing legs and extra eyes.
The buzzing of the bees grows quieter each year.

They ask, "How can you worry so much about animals?"
They say, "Our country needs oil.
They say, "Our country needs work.
They say, "Our country needs money."
They say, "We're number one."
They say, "God created man in his image."

But who are they?
And how do they know God?

I say,
"Sentinel species."
I say,

"The least of my brothers."
I say,
"Food chain."
I say,
"Science."

They say, "What is science?"
And they say, "I don't believe your scientists."
They say,
"Who are you?"
They say,
"Me, me, me."

So I ask you, "How do we work with them?"

ꙮ

Corinna's Cheek

By Jennifer Klein

Angel daughter.

As I bury my face against your neck
and tangle my hair in yours,
I feel your peach-soft cheek
so warm against mine.

You hug, squeezing so tightly,
and I smell your apple breath
as you murmur, "I love you, Mommy."

And I remember
to remember
this soft warm cheek
forever.

ꙮ

I Hope to Never Miss You

By Jennifer Klein

When a babe
with swollen new eyes
You looked at me
and made me yours.

I thought
How happy I am
And
How sad I would be
If ever I were to lose you.

Sometimes now I look out the window
to the woods
and I imagine us
Running from an unknown army.

So many have done so before us.
The Jews.
The Bosnian Muslims.
The Tutsis.

Sometimes I imagine
How your father
could ever chose
between death
and raping you.

"Never Again," they say
Until it happens again.

Now
I look at you
drawing at our kitchen table.
And I look at those quiet woods.

And I am thankful.
At least today,
At least in this place,
You are mine
To love completely.

ഇൽ

Burning the Past

By Dianalee Velie

Like a black butterfly boosted
by passionate ruby flames,

my charred personal identity
drifted into the evening sky,

floating with page after page
of her old address book,

pages having already succumbed
to the blaze in the roaring chiminea.

Red wine in our warming hands,
my friend continued to burn her past,

reciting a Litany of expletives:
dead, moved, lost all contact, also dead,

until she held my name in her hand,
and tossed the page on to the hearth,

where tongues of flames eagerly destroyed
my history to create the moment's warmth.

A truth, too simple to be spoken,
drifted into the evening air

with the delicate carbon filament, flitting
across the moon, disappearing among stars.

Published in The Pen Woman, September 2007
Gretchen Warren Award

ഇയ

Bad Date.com

By Dianalee Velie

The blue clown wig really didn't cut it,
nor did the big red balloon to really
mark his presence, but worse, the nit-wit
who kept his hat on to hide, least I see,

his total baldness. Better yet, a twelve-step
AA lecture while I choked on a glass
of wine inhibited any windswept
romance from occurring with this upper class

loner. Their edges blur, but extreme guilt
over a wife's suicide is not first date
conversation. Under that bed quilt
I dare not venture. I'd rather hibernate.

But one kudo to the man, who likes them fat
saying I'd look better in a 250-pound format.

ഌ

Exalting the X Chromosome

By Dianalee Velie

Clouds of creamy hydrangeas
and exuberant daisies
smiled to us from every room,
a calming womanly welcome
to this country farm house
where you placed the Adirondack
chairs in a semi-circle around
the outdoor fireplace,
a soft receptive curve, from you,
a woman we have never met.

On the worn wooden table inside,
we found bagels and bialys,
white fish from a Manhattan deli,
and homemade lox: gifts
so feminine of heart
they sheltered us under a canopy
of maternal love. Beneath this
protective aura, three sister travelers
lit the wood stove with the dry
split logs you had brought inside,

poured our libations and raised
our chalices to your presence,
exalting the X chromosome
with friendship and fine red wine.

ꕤ

Body Parts

By Dianalee Velie

Images of her ovaries float
before me on the doctor's screen,
the resting place of half the genetic
makeup of possible grandchildren
hidden in marshmallowy looking
orbs of potential parent.

Declared healthy, and accessible,
no shadows block the other genetic
half, linked to my son,
from completing their voyage,
their charge of desire,
and then division with purpose.

Purpose, what new purpose
do I possess as my own same
body parts wind slowly down?
Shrinking within me into little seeds
of longing, they stretch out their roots,
seeking streams of consciousness.

Never fearing drought,
fruitful, their stored energy
saturates me with insight,
and a welcoming hint
of wisdom: the conception
of dreams delivered.

ഇൽ

Domestication

By Dianalee Velie

My daughter-in-law thinks I've raised a gem:
her dear husband who loves to cook and clean,
my domestic skills an endearing emblem
of how I raised him. I smile, serene.

His laundry tasks are quite meticulous
and whites stay away from multi-color.
The bread is always perfect, ravenous
folks agree, whole grained and full of flavor.

My son, Mr. Wonderful, because of me?
Honestly, these traits I do not possess.
But I suspect the reason is simply
when he was eight, I now will confess,

I turned his white hockey stockings hot pink
and burned the bread as black as India-ink.

ഗ്ദ

ABOUT THE AUTHORS

Rhona Barlevy is an occupational therapist, potter, watercolorist and now a writer of short stories. She continues to be amazed at what comes out. Stay tuned—more is coming.

Marilou Barsam, with more than 25 years of experience in both traditional and online marketing, has contributed to Aspatore Books' marketing intelligence books, hosted numerous webcasts with business luminaries including Larry Weber, contributed regularly to BtoB's "Ask the Expert" online column, and contributed to other online publications/blogs, including her own: *My Educated Guess* and *The Informed Marketer*. She lives with her partner, Sarah, and daughter, Lily, in Bedford, MA.

Bob Beckwith: Following a career in direct marketing and sales, Bob wanted to try his hand at creative writing, purely for fun. Unlike his golf game, Bob found a wonderful writing coach, Mindy Pollack-Fusi, early on, thus avoiding the nurturing of bad habits.

Karen Bella currently lives in Belmont, MA and works at a hospital in a nearby city. She has been writing ever since she was little and can't imagine life without a pen and pad of paper. Writing will always be a way for her to work through different life situations.

Lisa Robin Benson is majoring in sculpture at the New York Academy of Art, where she is studying human anatomy, figure sculpture, clay modeling, and art history. She loves to read and write when she is not sculpting. You can see her sculptures, drawings and paintings at www.artisticobservations.com.

Charlotte Christen, retired librarian and lover of books, reading and writing, strives for brevity and simplicity in her life and in her writing, which has been predominantly non-fiction: personal essays, genealogical sketches, journal entries and bibliographic book annotations, but when so inspired, a poem or a children's story. The contributions to this book are her first attempts at adult fiction.

Linda Christen is a mother, potter, sociologist, community arts volunteer and advocate against sexual violence through her contributions to the Boston Area Rape Crisis Center, The Center for Hope and Healing in Lowell and by producing The Vagina Monologues in Bedford in February 2011. As a sociologist, Linda lost enthusiasm for writing—it was dull and seemed to flatten her topics, but through Mindy's classes, she is learning how to convey vibrancy and emotion in stories, essays, memoir and poems. Linda enjoys combining her academic and creative interests through pottery; her work can be seen in local galleries and at: lindaslocale.blogspot.com.

Claudia A. Fox Tree is a busy, happily single mom to five clever, creative, and curious teenagers whom she loves dearly. She has been a middle school special education teacher for almost 25 years, but still finds time to write, dance, craft clay jewelry, and go on adventures. Claudia is a multiracial American whose father is Native American (Arawak-Yurumein) and mother is German from Mannheim. To find out more about her multicultural work with social justice themes, see her blog: http://nativeamericanresources.blogspot.com/.

George L. Hand, PhD spent his working career as a rocket scientist. He has been married 55 years, has four great kids and ten grand kids. His latest interest is poetry, and he has written two self-published books.

Alma Hart, a social activist and Yankee immigrant, earned her Bachelor of Journalism from the University of Texas. She has lived in Bedford over twenty years with her family. She is currently completing her memoir, *Decoration Day*.

E.M. Karrick is an artist and poet who, with the inspiring help of Mindy Pollack-Fusi, decided to try her hand at creative story writing. "Kindergarten" and "The Wake" are her first two attempts.

Jennifer Klein is a former organic chemist and environmentalist who is now dedicating most of her time to raising her two wonderful daughters. She has always dreamed of being a fiction writer and was thrilled to meet Mindy just as her younger daughter started attending school full time. Finding Mindy and her writing classes and writing groups has been such a godsend to her.

Lea Ann Knight, CFP uses both sides of her brain, although rarely at the same time. When her left side is working, she dispenses financial advice in person, through her weekly blog, *Financially Fit After 40*, and as the Money Expert for Time Inc.'s *All You* magazine. When her right side gets a chance, she writes the *Fitch Tavern Tales*, a middle-grade historical mystery series, which can be explored at www.FitchTavernTales.com.

Susan Miele has a passion for organizational culture and design, change management and leadership development. She is currently enrolled in a doctoral program in Human and Organizational Systems at Fielding University. Susan loves to keep things interesting; she is a certified yoga instructor, nonprofit advocate and busy mom to a 12-year-old daughter.

The Rev. Dr. Bruce Nickerson, an ordained Episcopal deacon, grew up in Somerville and has published extensively. He and his wife, Joanna, live in Bedford, MA. His faith commitment, experiences, love of people living on the margins, and study of folklore result in "gut level" material about real people and situations, especially those we would like to ignore.

Katherine Picard is a retired community college Business and Office Administration professor. She has replaced writing lectures and exams with creative writing and memoir pieces. She also enjoys maintaining friendships, traveling, reading, and keeping up with her six grandsons.

Mindy Pollack-Fusi: Mindy coaches students' college application essays and teaches creative writing at The Place for Words, and writes freelance for *The Boston Globe.* She wishes to thank her mother for her writing and creative genes; her father for her entrepreneurial drive; Steve, Gina and Melissa for tolerating her crazy work hours; and Gilligan and The Skipper, for canine company while editing this book at the Cape. Contact her via www.ThePlaceforWords.com.

Louise St. Germain is a retired nurse. She and her husband have six children and fourteen grandchildren, which keeps her busy. Louise spends part of her retirement writing family stories and poems. Some of her works have been published. She currently leads a twice-monthly writers group at the Bedford Council on Aging. She can be reached at lstgermain@verizon.net.

Kathleen Shure is an artist/business owner with her husband and partner, Robert, of Skylight Studios, Inc. and the Giust Gallery. She is also an experienced registered nurse. Writing, for her, is a creative outlet and a fantastic journey into the unknown.

Dianalee Velie lives in Newbury, NH and is a frequent guest instructor at The Place for Words. She is a Sarah Lawrence College graduate, has a Master of Arts in Writing from Manhattanville College, and has taught poetry, memoir, and short story at universities, colleges and in private workshops. She is the author of *Glass House*, *First Edition*, *The Many Roads to Paradise*, and *Soul Proprietorship: Women in Search of Their Souls*. Her award-winning poetry and short stories have been published in hundreds of literary journals throughout the US and Canada. www.dianaleevelie.com

Judith Yarbrough is a retired registered pharmacy technician now working in an IP law firm. She is the "mother" of two beautiful cats, Molly and Maggie. Since childhood, Judith has written lots of short stories and has always wanted to be published.

Made in United States
North Haven, CT
16 May 2025